RAMA

— BY —

Jamake Highwater

REPLICA BOOKS

A DIVISION OF BAKER & TAYLOR
BRIDGEWATER, NJ

OTHER WORKS BY JAMAKE HIGHWATER

FICTION
Mick Jagger: The Singer Not the Song
Anpao
Journey to the Sky
The Sun, He Dies
Legend Days
The Ceremony of Innocence
I Wear the Morning Star
Eyes of Darkness
Kill Hole
Dark Legend

POETRY
Moonsong Lullaby
Songs for the Seasons

NONFICTION
Rock and Other Four Letter Words
Songs from the Earth: Native American Painting
Ritual of the Wind: Indian Ceremonies and Music
Many Smokes, Many Moons
Dance: Rituals of Experience
The Sweet Grass Lives On: 50 Indian Artists
The Primal Mind
Arts of the Indian Americas
Native Land, Sagas of American Civilizations
Shadow Show: An Autobiographical Insinuation
Myth and Sexuality
The Language of Vision

Rama

Rama
A Legend

JAMAKE HIGHWATER

With illustrations by
KELLI GLANCEY

HENRY HOLT AND COMPANY

New York

FOR BUCK

We are all in the gutter,
but some of us are looking at the stars.
— Oscar Wilde

Radiant as the sun, Rama came from his palace,
barefooted and valorous,
walking toward the open gates of heaven
with Vyavassaya, the goddess of the Earth,
ever close to his side.
— The Ramayana of Valmiki

Rama

The Kingdom

The darkness drops again; but now I know
That twenty centuries of stony sleep
Were vexed to nightmare by a rocking cradle,
And what rough beast, its hour come round at last,
Slouches towards Bethlehem to be born?

—William Butler Yeats

One

JT WAS A DEAD BODY!

Prince Rama cried out in astonishment when he saw the terrible sight.

It glowed with a mysterious green light. Some dreadful creature buried in the freshly turned soil. Something strange and forbidding.

The young prince peered intently into a deep furrow the farmers had carved into the ebony earth, dazed by what he saw. A graceful limb protruded from the ground. An arm. A delicate hand, its fingers curled into a voluptuous gesture, as if to beckon him.

The workmen who had uncovered the horrifying appendage muttered fearfully among themselves. They crouched next to Prince Rama, trembling with uncontrollable dread, but reluctant to retreat lest Prince Rama think them cowards.

Then there was a sound.

The farmers bolted, leaping into the air and shrieking as they desperately ran for cover.

The prince stood his ground, listening to the sound and leaning cautiously toward the arm that jutted out from the fissure in the earth. The sound was a strange, muffled song; drifting upward, rising like a distant echo from the naked, steamy soil, and carrying with it the archaic and misty stench of life and fertility.

From their hiding place, the farmers peered into the furrow, where fat red worms wiggled in the loose soil before they vanished into the crumbled loam.

"Dear Prince," one of them exclaimed, "go no closer to that evil thing! It is a trick to rob you of your power!"

Prince Rama ignored the warning and slowly stepped forward.

At just that moment, a ghastly shadow overtook the world. The sunshine fled as if it too feared the mysterious corpse buried in the upturned soil of the field.

In the ensuing darkness, the workmen cried out, whirling around to search the murky sky for the demon that had eaten the sun. Their eyes widened with horror as an immense tiger dashed across the horizon, turning first into a yellow cloud and then changing into a golden aurora of flame and sparks that roared and growled and disappeared into the turbid sky.

"Hush . . ." Prince Rama whispered, ignoring the fear of the farmers and slowly climbing down into the furrow, where he could get a better look at the delicate arm that rose from the ground.

"What evil thing is this?" he murmured. "What monster could have been so vile that it was buried here in common ground and denied a proper cremation?"

"Go no closer!" the farmers pleaded.

"Lord Rama, we beg of you! This place is cursed by wild women! Come away before it is too late!"

Rama gazed in amazement at the glowing arm as he kneeled beside it and began stealthily to scoop away earth with his hands.

Overcome by the shame of allowing their great lord to dig in the soil with his bare hands, the farmers hurried to Prince Rama's assistance, cringing at his side and apprehensively digging their fingers into the soft ground. They whimpered and glanced anxiously at one another as they burrowed into the place where they hoped to uncover the face of the buried creature.

Now Rama silently crouched beside them, expectantly watching their progress.

The song from the earth grew louder as the farmers dug. A soft green mist slowly spewed upward from the land, spreading across the fields and enveloping everything in its path as it turned the murky sky as luminous and verdant as a spring meadow.

Then one of the farmers gave out a squeal of terror, for he had brushed the soil away from what looked like a chin and the tip of a nose. Prince Rama quickly crawled toward the corpse and took up the task of uncovering the head, as the workman retreated with growing apprehension.

Rama gasped.

It was a human face.

A woman. A young and splendid woman. With exquisite brows and a voluptuous mouth. Her long, green hair tangled about her noble head.

"Quickly," Rama murmured, "we must uncover her at once. This is no demon. This young woman must be given a respectable cremation."

But the farmers were so stricken by anxiety that they could not do as their prince ordered.

With impatience and anger, Rama decided that he himself would rescue this poor woman from her lowly grave. He bent over the corpse, getting his legs firmly under him so he could grasp the woman by the arm and pull her from the dirt that covered her.

He carefully took her by the outstretched hand, and just as he was about to summon all of his strength to draw her from her humble grave, Rama bellowed with alarm.

"Help me!" he shouted to the farmers.

But it was too late.

The hand of the corpse moved! It slowly clutched his fingers, taking so firm a grasp that he could not pull free.

Now Prince Rama jolted upward, as if he had been struck by lightning. The farmers shrieked and fled, leaving him in the clutches of the dead woman.

Rama opened his mouth in agony, but he could not scream or shout. Blistering sparks burst all around him.

His eyes opened wide in horror and anguish. Streaks of green fire crackled and sped up his arm as he vainly tried to pull himself free of the hand that held him. He groaned. He wept. And then he arched back, staring into the sky. A terrible, long cry finally burst from his lungs. Reverberating endlessly across the fields. Until the green mist overtook him, and he fell. Collapsing. Falling. Plummeting into the soft, moist arms of the earth.

The green light went out.

And now there was nothing but silence and darkness.

Two

THE FORLORN CLANGING of gongs and cymbals rang out in the great chambers of the palace of King Dasaratha.

The long, slow cadence of drums resounded in the empty corridors, like a wounded giant mournfully stumbling through the underworld. One thousand candles flickered in the dim passageways, casting fleeting shadows into the smoke and incense-filled air. Offerings of fruit and flowers were laid at the feet of all the ferocious stone idols, whose bulging eyes stared out of animals' faces with long tusks and flared nostrils.

Chak-a-chak, chak-chak came the hypnotic voices of the temple dancers, moving in a trance, their arms rippling above their heads and their fingers delicately undulating in the clouds of incense. Silver bells jangling around their ankles and wrists. Prancing with naked feet and closed eyes through leaping flames, their faces filled with ecstasy as they walked obliviously upon fiery coals spread across the floor of the bejeweled sanctuary of King Dasaratha's palace. Giving their bodies to the fire so that their prince might be spared.

But death would not be appeased.

In the heart of the palace, the imperial mourners clustered anxiously around the bed of the king's favorite son, Prince Rama, weeping and chanting prayers, groveling on the floor and tearing at their hair, so great was their misery.

The drapes of the tall windows had been drawn closed, and in the dimness of the royal chamber there was nothing but lamentation and sorrow.

Rama lay upon his bed, pale, silent, and deathly still. Only the feeble and irregular heaving of his chest gave an indication that he might still be alive. But life was anxious to fly away, leaving nothing but a dark shadow where once there had been the magnificent bright light of the young prince's eyes.

Rama's brother, Laksmana, sat at his side, whispering desperately into Rama's ear, urging him not to give up his fight against death.

But Prince Rama did not stir.

The lamentation of the mourners grew louder as the evening approached and the dark wind that carries death in its mouth swirled into the savage sky. The clouds rolled back in terror. The creatures of the jungle crawled deep into their havens. And every living thing fled from the deadly messenger in the wind, leaving the world deserted and still, except for the night birds with shining yellow eyes that screeched and beat their massive wings, circling endlessly above the palace of King Dasaratha.

Far from the palace, in the humble village sprawled beneath the sacred mountain, peasant children heard the wailing of the mourners and the carnivorous cackle of the birds. Trembling with fear, they fled into the safety of their beds, shivering and moaning as the cold breath of death glided menacingly over their rooftops. Women turned down their lanterns. And old men cowered in dark corners, fearing that death might notice their decrepitude and sweep them under its heavy cloak of shining, black mirrors.

Rama lay helpless upon his bed, and there was nothing to be heard but wind and lamentations.

When, at last, the fearsome night had passed, and the sun made its blazing path along the bird-filled horizon, the drapes were drawn from the windows and the prince's room filled with sunlight. But still he did not stir.

Laksmana anxiously pressed his face to his brother's lips, and then he beamed with delight when he felt the wisp of Rama's fragile breath against his cheek.

"Still he lives!" Laksmana exclaimed with tears of gratitude.

But Prince Rama did not open his eyes nor did he respond when his brother gently called to him.

In desperation the great king summoned all the holy

ones and all the healers of his great domain. They hurried to his side from faraway places. From the deep jungle and the airless summit of the volcano, from the cave of the ancestors to the jagged rocks that rose from the sea of life in which the kingdom of Dasaratha floated. And when they were assembled in the palace, the king commanded them to achieve for Prince Rama what all the songs and dances of the priests could not achieve: to save his life.

But all their wisdom and all their magic was of no avail. Prince Rama lay pale and motionless. Alive but not alive. Balancing precariously upon that narrow brink of the world where light becomes darkness.

The days passed and still Rama would not come back into the world of the living. The endless drone of drums still filled the air. The slow palpitations of remorse and misery. The shrill lament of cymbals and chimes. And the worried nods of the king's wise men and medicine women. In this place of sorrow there were no other sounds. Only drums and the cymbals. Only the sighs of hapless people, resigned to the death of Prince Rama. Only night and day, as time made its merciless way through the great kingdom of Dasaratha.

And while time passed, the old king sat in gloom by the side of his young queen, Kekay-yee, staring off into space while he absently stroked her long black hair. When he spoke to her, his voice was barely a whisper. His ancient eyes searched into her lovely face for some sign of consolation. But the queen was still a child, a captive of war who had become the king's consort, too young and self-centered to understand her husband's apprehension for the life of his son. She knew nothing of the life that was lived beyond the palace gates. All she knew was that she was her husband's wife and the heir to his powerful realm. And though her sinister handmaïd, Kooni, implored the young queen to seize power from her husband's sons, she was too vain and proud to concern herself with anything but pleasure. And in her eyes was a trace of evil.

When Kekay-yee looked into the mirror, she saw only a lovely child sitting on the throne of a great queen. But she was not yet that great lady. For the real queen still lived. She was named Kowsalya, and it was she who had given King Dasaratha his two fine sons while she was still young and attractive. But now she was no longer the favorite of her royal husband. Her youth and beauty had vanished, and with the loss of her comeliness she had also lost the love of her husband.

So now young Kekay-yee was the first wife who sat beside King Dasaratha; while the old queen was banished to the corridors beyond the golden circle of the king's chambers, waiting in an endless twilight for some small word from her husband. Hunched over her silken tapestry, her fingers tirelessly embroidering the images of warriors and chariots . . . glorious depictions of her husband's youthful victories against the demons who dwelled in faraway lands.

But his glory days were over. The fearful illness of his son overwhelmed the king with exhaustion and remorse. No longer could he feel yearnings for victories and worldly power. Now there were only stillness and resignation in his heart as he gazed at his wounded son. Now there were only regret and contrition.

In the melancholy chamber where Prince Rama lay dying, the king staggered to his feet and crept toward his stricken son, falling to his knees and softly sobbing. Queen Kekay-yee dutifully following after him, bowing by his side, her face fixed in an expression of distress while her eyes were filled with indifference. A malicious butterfly ever fixed upon its own image. Something hideous hidden behind her mask of beauty.

The days of heroism and glory were over for the kingdom of Dasaratha. Now the war cries and victory dances had ended. And there were only the sighs of the hapless people. The world had changed. Nothing remained but starless nights and gloomy days, making their way through all the senseless circles of time.

Three

AT MIDNIGHT there came a rush of warm air down the corridors. Ten thousand candles flickered. Their flames sputtered and died, leaving nothing behind but darkness and whiffs of smoke.

The drums were silent. The clatter of cymbals and chimes suddenly ceased. For a moment, the people assembled around the dying prince held their breath, fearful that Rama had left them forever.

In that terrible silence, the great doors of the chamber burst open and the elderly queen, Kowsalya, rushed into the room.

"You can keep me from my son no longer!" she exclaimed, whirling to face the king, a fierce expression in her radiant eyes. "If you will not allow me to be his mother, at least let me be his nurse!"

Laksmana embraced his mother, ready to protect her from the aggression of the young queen, who despised her. Then he turned to his father, the king, and implored, "Leave her in peace! I beg you, Father, let my mother stay with us to mourn my dear brother and her dearest son!"

But King Dasaratha was not persuaded. He was about to command Queen Kowsalya to leave them, but she pulled free of the protective arms of her son and frantically advanced upon the king.

"Before he dies!" she shouted. "Before you let Rama die, you must let me use what little power I still have to snatch him away from death!" she pleaded. "I am old and my face no longer pleases you, but I beg of you: let me be his nurse! I still possess the one thing in all the world that can save Rama!" she declared.

The wise men muttered amongst themselves and scoffed with indignation. "If any power on earth could save Prince Rama, we would possess that power!"

"But you lack the one gift that I possess," whispered the elderly queen.

"And what power is that?" the wise men demanded arrogantly.

"*It is called love,*" she murmured as tears came into her eyes. "He is my child. And I love him more than I love my own life."

The hostile assembly of wise men fell silent, shamed by Queen Kowsalya's gentle words.

"Rama is the river that flows from me," she wept as she clutched her belly and bent low, as if her entire body were afflicted by the deadly malady that was slowly stealing her son's energy. "He is the life that I will live when I can live no more. He is the sunshine of ten thousand days I shall never see. He is the gentle man who was the gentle boy. The helpless child who became the virtuous man. The same lips as those small lips that suckled at my breast. The tiny fingers that clutched my arms. The boy who learned to fight his enemies with tears in his eyes. The man who is my son."

The elderly queen bowed in grief. And now in the great chamber there was only the sound of her labored breathing. In the stillness, she cautiously approached the king and, kneeling at his side, she hesitantly reached out and lightly touched his wrinkled hand.

At once young Queen Kekay-yee recoiled in rage, rising to her feet defiantly as she gave her husband a disapproving look. "If you intend to give an audience to this old woman," she hissed, "then I shall withdraw and find far happier company elsewhere!"

Then she turned to leave the royal chamber.

"Stay . . . stay," the king pleaded. "Stay and give me a moment's peace in all my affliction," he entreated, looking at both of his wives with impatience and exhaustion. "Must the two of you forever conspire to make my life a misery?" he complained.

Then he gave his young wife a desperate look and said: "If it can help Rama, surely you will allow Kowsalya to speak."

The young queen cast a dark glance at her rival,

scowling with childish resentment as she reluctantly resumed her position next to her husband. "Since you insist," Kekay-yee muttered, tossing back her long black hair, "I will stay and she will speak. But let her waste no time. Let her say whatever she must say, and then let her be on her way back to her solitude!"

The king took a deep breath, raising his trembling fingers to his head as if the strife between his wives and the fate of his favorite son were a terrible weight upon his brow. "Tell me, then," he whispered to his elder wife, gazing questioningly into her aged face, "what help is there for our poor son? What miracle do you possess that can save him?"

The queen leaned very close to her husband's ear, and then she whispered, "There is but one magic great enough to break the spell that holds Rama prisoner, and that magic can only be found in a faraway kingdom."

"But where is such a kingdom?" Dasaratha exclaimed. "Tell me and I shall conquer it at once and steal its magic!"

"It is a lie!" shouted the wise men. "There is no such kingdom! There is no such magic!"

Queen Kowsalya dismissed the retort of the ministers and leaned even closer to the king's ear, whispering: "It is a kingdom far beyond the valley of the moon. Across the burning river that runs like blood. Beyond the mountain that spits fire. In the land of the great eagle called Garuda. And beyond the cave of the white demons that devour the bones of children lost in the dark. Beyond all that is known to us. It is to be found only there . . . on a lake of lights and in the mysterious palace of King Janaka."

The wise men recoiled in horror. "How can you speak his name? King Janaka is a fiend! He is no better than a monster!" they shouted.

The medicine women and ministers howled with revulsion. "He eats the flesh of swine and drinks the blood of falling stars!"

At this, even the king covered his ears in dread.

Queen Kekay-yee had listened to the debate with malicious delight. "What a fool this old woman is!" she gloated, mockingly prancing around the elderly queen. "She wants you to take poor Rama to the den of monsters!"

Undaunted, the older queen ignored the taunts of Kekay-yee and clung to her husband's side, imploring him to listen to her words.

"When I was still young and as beautiful as a new moon . . ." she told him, "in those happy days, long forgotten, my handmaid was a silent little creature named Kara. It was she who told me of the land from which she had been stolen, a strange and wondrous place called Janaka. From the very first day she came into my service, she longed to be set free so she could return to her own country."

"All this I know!" the king exclaimed impatiently. "You

forever begged for her freedom, but I would not let her go. So what good to us is your slave?"

"It is her magic that we need," the queen murmured, making a mysterious gesture with her hands. "But first we must find her."

The wise men laughed mockingly. "Find her? But foolish lady, she is long dead. You yourself reported her death to all of us many years ago."

"She lives!" the queen insisted with wide eyes and trembling hands. "She did not die. I sent her away. The day came when it was time for her to leave. Her magic had kept my husband close to my side. But many years passed, and the darkness of time began to fall across the full moon of my youth, overtaking me like a shadow, until all that was left was a silver crescent in the indifferent eyes of my husband. The king no longer gazed at me in wonderment and love. He no longer called the flute players to our bedchamber. And I found myself alone, with my handmaid Kara as my only companion. She and I grew old together. Captives in the same palace; prisoners of the same sunless chambers. I, a queen, and she a slave. Yet with old age we had become the same . . . sorrowful women burdened by grief. One gloomy morning I awakened and found my old age lying beside me, like a fatal malady that had overtaken my body while I slept. I covered all the mirrors of my chamber. I burned my bridal robes. And then I summoned faithful Kara and told her she was free. How she

21

embraced me! How she kissed my cheek! And then, without a word, she vanished down the narrow path that climbs toward the valley of the moon. I have never seen her again. But I know that she still lives, and I know that she loves our son Rama. It is she who will allow us to enter the invincible and mysterious palace of King Janaka."

King Dasaratha sighed heavily and shook his head as he gazed with pity at his old wife. "But dear lady, tell us: what can this enemy and monster-king possibly do to help Rama?"

"It is not the king but his daughter who possesses the magic that can save Rama!" Kowsalya exclaimed. "This I know, for Kara often told me of that daughter's great powers!"

The wise men murmured with fear and cowered at the queen's words. "They say she is a sorceress . . . a creature who sleeps in a bed of earth and eats only leaves and berries!" one voice wailed.

"They say she is a great beauty with marvelous black eyes and long tassels of green hair. More at home in the jungle than in the palace of her father!" another voice exclaimed.

"They say that whatever she touches dies!"

"Or lives! For she has the greatest of all powers! The power of life and death!" the queen insisted. "She can speak to the rivers and the mountains, and when they hear her, they shake winter from their backs and open their arms to endless springtime. It is she who has the magic to revive Rama from his deathly slumber!"

"No! No! No!" the wise men and medicine women shouted, while young Queen Kekay-yee laughed, her mouth slowly twisting into a demonic smile.

Only Laksmana was willing to defend his mother. He embraced Queen Kowsalya and shouted: "She has been made wise by love! And I believe that she speaks the truth!"

The king raised his arms, demanding silence. He slowly arose from his throne and, listless, walked the full length of the great hall. He paused by the bed where his son lay motionless and ashen, surrounded by magicians and wizards chanting prayers and incantations.

After a long silence, he turned to Queen Kowsalya and said: "Rama must live. That much I know. But I am an old warrior who knows little of wizardry and sorceries. And yet, if this terrible King Janaka has a daughter who can save Rama with her magic, then we must find her. So tell me, quickly, dear lady, what is this demon daughter's name?"

Queen Kowsalya did not respond. She gazed anxiously across the great distance that separated her from her husband, and as she slowly brought her hands to her breasts, she began to weep.

In the silence, King Dasaratha slowly drew close to Rama's bed and gently touched the young man's hand.

"Her name?" the king repeated in a loud voice. "Tell me, woman, what is this demon's name?"

There was an anguished rumble that rose from the earth. The queen gasped and clutched her throat in horror.

Silence.

Then, softly from the distance, the air stirred with the fragile echo of chimes and cymbals. A warm breeze swept through the dark corridor and into the great hall. Suddenly ten thousand candles magically ignited, and their delicate blue flames danced in the dark.

The queen moved her lips, but no sound came from them. She peered anxiously into the air, shuddering with fear, as if she could not bring herself to pronounce the word. Then, after a long and fearsome silence, the queen muttered in a voice that was more a groan than a whisper: *"Her name is Sita."*

Now there was a terrifying roar, as if a mountain had fallen upon the palace. It was a blast so powerful that it shook the massive stones of the great walls. Echoing again and again in the ears of the assembly.

SITASITASITASITASITASITA!

The wizards at Rama's deathbed cried out in horror, cowering in terror.

"Look!" they shouted.

Rama's arm slowly rose from his side and clutched the empty air. At the same moment, an intense green light burst into the chamber.

The young queen screamed.

The deceitful wizards fell to the floor, writhing as they were consumed by the green fire. Burning. Transformed into sparks that vanished into the night.

Silence again.

Then the long, low beating of the drums, like the pounding of a human heart.

Prince Rama bolted upward, miraculously rising to his feet as if he had been dragged out of his grave. At the sight of Rama's glowing figure, even the wise men fell back in fear.

Rama opened his mouth, but there was no sound. Blistering flames burst all around him. His blank eyes opened wide. Streaks of green fire crackled in his hair and crackled up and down his body. Then he arched back, staring into nothingness, until a long cry for help burst from his lungs. A pathetic screech that reverberated through the great halls and corridors of the palace.

Rama staggered, trying to stay on his feet, but the green mist overtook him, and he fell.

Now the light went out. The candles flickered and died. And the chamber was plunged into darkness.

In the shadows, the king covered his eyes in amazement as Rama's limp body pulsated and glowed in the dark.

"Now do you believe what I have told you?" the elder queen whispered as she fell to her knees, weeping at the side of her son.

"Yes . . ." the king whimpered in a choked voice, "now I believe."

Then he turned and announced in a strong voice full of urgency: "It is decided. We must go at once to the palace of King Janaka."

Four

EVERYWHERE in the world of the night. The sounds of flutes and falling water.

Everywhere moonlight and starlight intertwined.

Moving. Moving. Rama was being carried through an endless landscape. He stared upward through blank eyes. Seeing a tapestry of leaves, shot through with bursts of light. Moon and starlight intertwined.

He was entombed somewhere deep within his own body. Lost within himself, in a solitary place full of darkness. A place in the interior of his mind, far beyond his speechless lips and motionless limbs. Entangled in himself. A fragile bird in a net. Unable to awaken from a dreadful sleep. Trapped and buried alive in his own body. Seeing sky. Only seeing. Faces. Tears. His brother, Laksmana, tormented by grief, looking down at him. His father, gray with misery and distress. Then the face of his weeping mother. Hovering over him, begging him to speak, though he could no longer

speak. Begging him to live, though he could no longer
live.

Moving. Moving. Carried endlessly beneath a canopy
of dreams. Assailed by colors and sounds. Alert and
alive, but unable to stir. Submerged in himself, without
movement or mortality. Breathing but dead. Peering out
at a world he could not reach. Unseen and unheard, like
a prisoner squinting through a tiny crack in the massive
walls of his prison. Watching helplessly as he was carried over crooked paths and through snarls of undergrowth and thick jungle, and then far beyond the valley
of the moon.

Everywhere.

Still the sound of flutes and falling water.

Everywhere moonlight and starlight intertwined.
Night upon night. Endless winter in his heart, while all
around was an endless springtime.

And in the sweet air, lacy trees that had never known
the frost of winter. Feathery leaves. Slender branches
spreading wide. Leafy skies filled with azure blossoms
and scarlet birds singing their secret songs.

Everywhere the glimmer of a strange illumination,
pierced by the trembling wings of one million jade
butterflies, fluttering aimlessly through a sky lighted
now both by sun and moon. And overhead, a trillion
emerald stars casting their luminous beadwork against
colossal purple clouds.

Everywhere the swift and somber songs of enchantment. The jungle's dark and ever-watchful eyes. The pale mist that forever listened. Sorceries and magic among the cobwebs and the shadows. Whispered spells that transformed the yellow flowers into swarms of black moths that filled the air, obliterating the sun and moon, and guarding the dangerous, narrow passage that led from the valley of the moon to the fantastic kingdom of Janaka.

Then suddenly everything stopped.

A strange voice was heard.

"Kahhh," it growled, more like a beast than like a human being.

Again the voice.

"Kahhh! Hurry with him! You must take him to her who is SHE! Hurry! Take him to the great one!"

Moving. Moving.

Carried recklessly through dark chambers and narrow corridors. Torches. Dancing flames. Smoke. Bats flitting in the shadows. Bats and wide-eyed monkeys hanging from the ceilings. Everywhere. Everywhere monkeys and lizards and black snails, clinging to the wet stone ceiling that loomed over him.

Bells. Chimes. And his heart, beating in the rhythm of the temple drums. Beating so fast and furiously that he felt dizzy with the pounding of the life imprisoned within him. Faster and faster the drumming of his heart, until he could see nothing and he could hear nothing but the faint whispers of his existence reverberating in helpless circles inside his lightless skull.

When at last he opened his eyes, he could see a ferocious creature hovering over him: purple skin, knotted hair, the breasts of a woman, and the motley whiskers of an old man. Tiger eyes. Tiger eyes and tiger teeth. And now the hot, moist breath of its narrow black lips blowing softly against his cheek.

Drum . . . drum . . . drumming him. Sending him into an appalling sleep.

Five

A FRAGRANT BREEZE swept over him. Fertile and fresh. A cascade of warmth and mist. Then a powerful spasm suddenly took hold of him, shaking his spirit and awakening him from extinction.

All at once, as the beating of drums surrounded him with their joyous rhythms, he could hear himself breathing. And in his breath he could hear the sound of grass growing. The groan of blossoms bursting into bloom. The ancient sigh of lands and rivers. Drumming. Everywhere life's anxious drumming. The steady pulse and warmth of an embrace that enveloped him with its massive throbbing.

He drew a deep breath and shuddered as a tide of sensation slowly crept through his senseless body. Then an intense pain twisted his limbs, gripping him with throbbing convulsions until he was liberated and sent into the world with a cry of life, like a child born of its mother.

When, at last, Rama opened his eyes, he stared into an

endless sky filled with sunshine. Vast emptiness immersed in a brilliant light. Then, for just an instant, he caught sight of a fantastic creature flitting over him: a young woman so beautiful that her image flashed upon his eyes like a streak of lightning. Then, as quickly as she appeared, her glorious face, surrounded by ornaments and garlands of flowers, darted out of view, melting into the bright light.

"Wait . . ." he murmured in a feeble voice, trying to stop her from leaving.

But Rama was too weak to speak or to rise. And when he called after the young woman, it was his brother, Laksmana, who appeared, smiling down at him with intense gratitude for the miracle of his recovery.

"That woman . . ." Rama whispered, finding his voice in the deathly silence that still lived within his chest and throat. "Who is that woman?"

Laksmana gently embraced his brother, murmuring: "Rest. Rest yourself. There is no woman. There is no one here but you and me and our dear mother."

Rama was too weak to challenge his brother's words. So, with a gentle sigh, he lay back and slowly closed his eyes, reluctant to give up the sunshine he had rediscovered after narrowly escaping from the grasp of death.

In a few days, when Rama's energy finally returned to him, he laboriously arose from his bed with the tender help of his brother, who held him like a newly born infant, until Rama could hesitantly take his first un- assisted steps. His mother, Kowsalya, hugged him with thankful tears, offering up abundant benedictions to the magical powers that had brought her son back from the land of the dead. But Rama himself remembered noth- ing. Not the fateful encounter with the mysterious corpse his workmen had unearthed in the royal pastures. Not his long illness. Not the arduous journey to the kingdom of Janaka and the meeting with his mother's servant, Kara. Not even the enchanted rituals that had saved him.

All he could remember was the incredibly beautiful face of the woman he had seen upon awakening from death.

"There was no woman," Laksmana insisted playfully. "It is just wishful thinking, dear Rama!"

"Laksmana is right," Kowsalya affirmed. "We alone watched over you while you slept the sleep of death. So this woman you saw . . . she must have been a sweet dream."

"If you had seen anything," King Dasaratha assured his son, "then it would have been something terrible beyond description."

With this, the king shuddered, saying in a voice full of fear and wonder, "You are lucky if you remember noth- ing. Forgetfulness is the blessing of your cure. For as you lay helpless in the care of a sorceress, all there was to see was a horrible creature, dripping with slime and muck. I myself had but a glimpse of that awful beast, and I was stung to the heart by fear at what I saw as they carried you into a dark and gloomy cave despite all my objections," he vividly recalled. "It was only then, as they rolled a great stone into the entrance, that I caught sight of a shadow descending upon you. A monster like none I have known. And I cried out for fear of never seeing you in this world again!"

"I tell you," Rama insisted as he and his family walked along the lofty terraces of the palace of King Janaka, "what I say is true. *There was a woman.* And I shall never forget her face!"

His mother, Queen Kowsalya, smiled cheerfully at Rama. "Perhaps she is your spirit wife," she mused.

"I think perhaps my poor brother is in love!" Laksmana teased.

But King Dasaratha was solemn. "Let us hope he is in love with a real woman and not a spirit, for he will need a good wife to sit beside him when I am too old to occupy the throne of our vast kingdom!"

Despite the chatter of his family, Rama could hear none of their comments, so great was his preoccupation with the memory of the creature he had first seen upon opening his eyes. He was so captivated by the image of the spirit woman that he hardly took notice of the mighty treasures of Janaka that spread in every direction.

He trailed aimlessly after his family members as they were given a grand tour of the palace. He nodded absently when their royal escorts pointed out the arena where ferocious elephant fights were in progress. He hardly took notice of the massive beasts as they butted and lunged at one another, cheered by crowds of exuberant young Janakan men. Nor did he take any interest in the groups of handsome young women, singing and dancing to the accompaniment of bells and drums, when they smiled at Rama and Laksmana, whispering to one another about the good-looking lads who were strangers in the land of Janaka.

Laksmana flashed a brilliant smile at the women, and he playfully nudged Rama. But Rama was not interested. Though he glanced at the girls, he did not see them, for he was blinded by the memory of the spirit woman.

The tour was long, and the elderly king Dasaratha and his queen Kowsalya leaned heavily upon the attendants who accompanied them, strolling across a bridge of silver that arched over a glimmering pool filled with fishes of many colors that glided continually in intertwining circles. They wandered through translucent corridors of rare onyx, where a warm breeze showered them with cascades of fragrant rose petals. Then they ventured out upon wide balconies where white peacocks flaunted their magnificence as they disdainfully cleared a path for the royal visitors.

In the open air, the sun was fierce. Queen Kowsalya

raised her hand to shield her eyes from the brightness, and at once attendants rushed forward with brightly colored umbrellas of silk to shade King Dasaratha and his family.

King Dasaratha took note of these many courtesies and whispered to Rama, "Despite my suspicions of King Janaka, there can be no doubt that our royal host wishes to grant us his unlimited hospitality."

After a leisurely tour of the palace of Janaka, the guests reached the grand assembly hall, with its gleaming turrets of gold and bejeweled walls. Here, at last, they were to meet the mysterious and dreaded King Janaka in order to present him with gifts and deep gratitude for Rama's miraculous recovery.

They were greeted in the royal chamber with much ceremony. Five hundred white doves were released from their cages and fluttered into the vast vaulted heights of the throne room. Ten thousand lanterns flickered in the shadows. Everywhere dazzling garlands hung from the porticos. And smiling people were everywhere. Ministers bowed low to them. Soldiers stood respectfully tall. And beautiful naked children ran in circles and covered their eyes in a ritual gesture of veneration.

The drums began to sound and long lines of warriors marched solemnly forward, carrying bright pennants and elegant standards encrusted with jewels and adorned with long ribbons and thousands of tiny silver bells that filled the air with their shimmering music.

King Dasaratha and his family watched expectantly for the appearance of the celebrated king of Janaka, not knowing what kind of a creature to expect, for no one from Dasaratha had ever set eyes on this strange and mysterious monarch, though in every valley and in the depths of the jungle people spoke of him with fear and forboding. Even King Dasaratha, despite all his greatness and power, was awed by both apprehension and excitement as the assembly hall slowly filled with nobles and princes, priests and warriors, and choruses of sacred dancers and musicians, beating their drums, striking their cymbals, and blowing upon their bamboo flutes and conch trumpets. All awaiting the grand entrance of King Janaka.

Then there was a deep silence. Only a low murmur came from the great throng as people bowed their heads and a huge copper door silently swung open. All those assembled in the hall, except King Dasaratha and his family, fell to their knees, averting their eyes and adoringly pressing their palms to the earth as they whispered incantations unknown to the visitors.

Now again silence.

Into this hushed and devout assembly walked a man, smiling at some jest that only he understood. A little man. A simple man without crown or scepter. His large head was bare and his hands were empty except for a humble sprig of wheat, which he carried with the solemnity of a sacred relic. He was a congenial man with large eyes and short legs. A man who looked more like a peasant than a king, dressed in tatters and rags.

When King Dasaratha saw this insignificant, stubby little man striding toward him, he became enraged, believing that he was the brunt of a vicious joke.

How could this dwarf possibly be the dreaded and infamous king of great Janaka?

Just as King Dasaratha was about to protest in humiliated rage, he became aware of something very curious. Though the shabby man approaching him seemed to be walking like any other creature, when King Dasaratha looked down at the floor, he realized that the little fellow's feet did not once touch the ground. He seemed to float, like a swimmer treading deep water, hovering upon a silver mist and held aloft by some power that seemed to pulsate and glow in the shaft of wheat he held in his delicate hand.

While King Dasaratha fell back in astonished wonder, his queen smiled with complete acceptance of her host's fantastic appearance. She bowed low to the monarch of Janaka, who returned her reverent greeting as he gently took the lady's hand.

"We welcome our brothers and sisters of Dasaratha," King Janaka sang out in a voice that trilled like the call of a bird.

Then he presented the sprig of wheat to Queen Kowsalya, who accepted it without hesitation, despite the whispered cautions of her flustered husband. At once, a marvelous radiance darted from the wheat, glowing in the queen's hand and permeating her entire body. The slouch of her shoulders vanished. Her limbs grew strong and handsome and lean. And into her haggard face came a springtime so youthful and warm that King Dasaratha gasped in amazed joy. Now he knew without a doubt that this inconspicuous little man in rags was surely the renowned and enigmatic monarch of Janaka.

Recovering his composure, King Dasaratha formally presented his sons to the dwarfish monarch, who greeted Rama and Laksmana with keen interest.

He leaned close to the ear of Queen Kowsalya and asked, "And where are the wives of your princely sons?"

"They are not yet married, sire," the queen responded as she and the little king exchanged a knowing smile.

"Ah," trilled King Janaka. "How good it is to have fine children, my lady. I know that pleasure well. So, without delay, let me present to you my one and only child."

Then King Janaka drew his tattered cloak around his shoulders, turning slowly toward the darkest corner of the vast chamber.

"Daughter," King Janaka sang out tunefully with a long and vibrant warble, "come from the deep, my child, and meet our distinguished visitors."

Then there was a sound.

The assembled people of the court hesitantly raised

their eyes for the first time since the arrival of their king. Then they turned toward the darkness and murmured in low and reverent voices.

"*Sita*. Divine Sita comes."

There was a harrowing, low growl, like the sound of a beast about to attack.

King Dasaratha and Laksmana drew back in fear, but Rama and his mother stood their ground, leaning cautiously toward the murky corner from which the sound emanated.

It was a strange, muffled sound: drifting upward, rising like a distant echo from the naked stones of the palace. Now a shadow overtook the chamber. In the ensuing dimness, a slender figure slowly emerged from the green mist that emanated from the massive stone walls.

Rama gasped with delight and wonder.

Standing before him was the glorious woman he had seen in his dreams.

King Janaka smiled lavishly and trilled: "Dear ladies and gentlemen, I wish to present to you my lovely daughter. Though in truth she is not my real daughter, for I am alone both in life and in death, having neither wife nor child. But fortunately for me, one day while plowing the earth in the sacrificial grove, the blade of my plow uncovered a marvelous creature and she became my only daughter and heir. I call her Sita. And Sita she will be, for she came to me from the furrow I was tracing in the rich and sacred earth, and that is the meaning of her name."

Rama stumbled forward, crying out, "I must speak to her!"

But King Janaka restrained him.

"Wait, my boy. Go no closer! What you ask is impossible. For you may not speak to Sita. This child, born from the soil, is a marvel and a delight, but, sad to say, she is mute and will remain silent until the day that she is both revered and loved by someone who is worthy of her."

Rama gazed at Sita with great longing. She glistened like a lotus just opening to the evening, rising above the calm water upon the pedestal of one perfectly oval leaf: her white flesh, her flawless body, and her enchanting face crowned by long tresses of emerald hair. She hovered in the green mist that surrounded her, swaying gently as crystal chimes resounded in cascades of shimmering music. She was close but far, her eyes glazed and her glance remote, looking out at the world as if she were not quite a part of it, as if she and Rama stood at a great distance from each other. Silent and immobile, like a statue of glass and light.

Rama trembled with expectation, never taking his eyes from her, stupefied by a strange and wonderful scent that overwhelmed his senses with its voluptuous mingling of herbs and blossoms and tender roots.

Then as suddenly as she had appeared, Sita turned away and vanished into the green mist.

Six

"FOR THE MARRIAGE of my daughter," explained King Janaka, slowly sitting upon his humble throne of bamboo and raffia, "it was declared by me and made known to all the great rulers and princes seeking her hand that I would bestow Sita only on that man whose excellence was confirmed by an exceptional task. But it was a task unlike any they had ever faced," King Janaka whispered with a winsome grin. "For, unbeknown to those who crowded this very chamber to attempt the task, it was not a test of manly strength and virility, but a far greater test of the spirit!"

Rama and Laksmana were enthralled by the king's curious story, and they leaned forward and listened with great interest. But their father, the old king of Dasaratha, was exhausted, and he peacefully dozed upon a huge and downy pillow; while his queen amused herself by peering at her recovered youth in an ornate mirror.

"And what came of this test?" asked Rama.

"Yes, tell us. What happened to those who undertook the test?" urged Laksmana.

"Many great and distant princes and monarchs came here to compete for Sita's hand," King Janaka murmured enticingly as he slowly moved his small hands in a hypnotic pantomime of his tale. "Yes, indeed, the entire countryside was filled with magnificent caravans and royal retainers. There were brutal soldiers and ruthless warriors with their barbarous weapons. There were poets and troubadours. Craftsmen and peasants."

King Janaka's somber expression suddenly changed, and he rubbed his hands together with mischievous delight. "They came expecting to fight a monstrous king! A monster and a fiend!" He laughed. "They approached with great intrepidity, drums blasting and trumpets blaring, expecting to find an army of terrifying demons! For they had heard ghastly stories from the cowards who had failed the test: stories of an unspeakably horrid brute named King Janaka! They gave any excuse they could imagine in order to explain their failure to succeed at the test I put before them!" the little king exclaimed with peals of laughter. "Can you imagine! They told such big lies that all the world became afraid of me!" he bellowed, throwing up his little arms as he laughed uncontrollably. "But what they really feared were the childish stories they invented about vile sorceries. About an imaginary tyrant . . . that bloodthirsty madman of Janaka and his vast armies of loathsome fiends!" King Janaka howled as great tears of mirth flowed from his sparkling little eyes.

He could barely catch his breath, so great was King Janaka's glee. Then, when his laughter finally subsided, he gazed with an expression of serenity at Rama and Laksmana, saying in a humble voice: "But you see, my friends, there is no fiend. No armies. No terrifying villains. Only me. Just this little old man whom you have found here in our tranquil and happy kingdom of Janaka."

Rama and Laksmana smiled at each other and sighed with great admiration for the mild-mannered and jovial king of Janaka.

In turn, the little king grinned back at them, wiping the tears of laughter from his gentle eyes and taking a deep and contented breath.

Now he slipped from the edge of his miniature throne and playfully crept toward his visitors, dancing on his stubby legs as he continued his story in a bumbling little ritual of chirped phrases and birdish gestures.

"Gradually," he sang in his warbling voice, "the lies of those who had failed the test became more fearsome and powerful than all the armies of the world. And day by day, the lies about me built a great wall of dread around Janaka . . . a wall that only the most foolish or the most holy of people dared to approach. So now, my young friends, we must try to find out if you are fools or righteous and holy men."

"My lord . . ." Laksmana began, starting to praise the many virtues of his brother, but King Janaka raised his hand for silence.

"Be patient, my friends. There is ample time for you to prove yourselves. But for now, my story is not yet ended," the king gently counseled.

Then he shook his round, bald head in an expression of sorrow.

"Alas," he murmured, "my story ends in calamity. For my enemies have no compassion. They are driven by their ambition and rage. Anger is their only amusement. And I have learned that angry men are tireless in their anger. So great was the rage of Sita's failed suitors that they created a monster of me. But my dear young friends, just look at me. I am such a humble little king. What harm could I do to such mighty monarchs as those who oppose me? And yet my wrathful foes were so shamed by their failure to win Sita that they turned me into a monster."

Now King Janaka's large eyes filled with tears. And he touched Rama lightly upon the shoulder.

"But no matter their aggression and their threats," the threadbare little king murmured sadly, "still I have refused to bestow my daughter upon any of them. And so, one day, they surrounded my defenseless kingdom and inflicted great hardships upon my lands and my people. The sun hid from us. The rain fled into the east. And the green mist of springtime that eternally graces our happy

45

world could not find its way into our skies. I feared that there would be an end to all of us. And then, one deep night of the dark of the moon, my mute and magnificent daughter emerged from her bed of earth, and with one wave of her delicate hand, she brought drought and famine to our enemies. They hastily retreated to their homelands, only to find all they had possessed now devastated. All they had loved now vanished from the good earth. No water flowed into their rice fields. No ginger or cinnamon grew upon their lands. Their goats lay down and would give no milk. And the mango groves were beset by ferocious tigers that preyed upon their people but would not harm their lambs. So it always is with people who live with anger. The sweet grass will not grow for them."

The king fell silent as he returned to his throne, where he sat hunched over in deep thought.

In the silence only the gentle snoring of old King Dasaratha could be heard.

Queen Kowsalya, long roused from her reveries by King Janaka's thrilling story, finally broke the silence.

"My sons are good men," she murmured as she approached the throne. "Will you not test their valor and spirit?"

"Yes!" Laksmana exclaimed. "Let my brother and me attempt what all others have failed to achieve!"

King Janaka laughed softly, looking warily at the

eager young men. "Tell me," he whispered, "are you driven by anger or by compassion?"

Laksmana answered at once: "I am driven by courage!"

Then the little king glanced at Rama and awaited his reply.

After a very long silence, Rama gazed into the mist where he had last seen the exquisite woman named Sita, and then he slowly whispered: "I am driven by love."

At these words, the humble king's eyes lighted with an incredible glow. He smiled wisely to himself, and then he proclaimed: "Then let it be done!"

At once a fresh, strong gust of wind whirled through the chamber, bringing with it, like leaves in a storm, countless sentries and nobles, priests and curious creatures that were neither men nor animals. A bright, crystalline music resounded. Cloud bells and lightning cymbals crackled and clattered, filling the air with their clamor. The massive walls of the palace slowly glistened, becoming as translucent as glass and allowing a torrent of dazzling light to flood the throne room.

Everywhere there were the excited voices of the countless beings who had mysteriously appeared, forming a teeming assembly of anxious spectators. But when King Janaka raised his arms, they respectfully lowered to their knees and fell silent.

"These two young men of Dasaratha, Laksmana and Rama, wish to undertake the ordeal that all others have failed," the king announced in a voice so loud that even the old monarch of Dasaratha stirred from his deep sleep, snorting in surprise and gazing with puzzlement at the great throng that now surrounded him.

"So I bid you to sound the drums and herald the occasion so the priests will bring to us the most sacred of things in our kingdom!" King Janaka continued. "Bring me the Tiger Bow, the power of which is unequaled in all the world. Unveil the bow, made of the wood of the giant banyan tree, so Rama and Laksmana may try their skill. And if one of them is able to lift the magic bow, then I will bestow my daughter, Sita, in marriage to that man!"

An exuberant shout rang out from the crowd. People threw brightly colored blossoms and fragrant rice into the air. The drums roared as the priests spilled precious wine upon the stone floor, marking the path of a procession of petite temple dancers, wrapped in rich gold brocades and adorned with flowers and jewels. Their long slender fingers undulated as they floated forward and their eyes were glazed and spellbound. Their gorgeous headdresses were fashioned from wreaths of silver, festooned with frangipani blooms and dangling with tinkling bells.

Then the trance dancers careened through the crowd, snarling and wheeling hypnotically as they thrust their ivory-crowned daggers into their breasts, opening wide but bloodless wounds.

Everywhere there was shimmering music and the ceaseless chanting of men: *"Ait! Aes, aes, byok, sirrr! Cak . . . cak . . . cuk!"*

Then came long processions of women carrying tall, swaying pennants made of palm leaves and orchid garlands, followed by the honored elders holding lofty silken umbrellas wrapped in saffron cloth and colored raffia.

At the end of the long procession were five hundred burly men who staggered forward, barely able to draw the eight-wheeled cart on which the iron box containing the Tiger Bow was placed.

The boisterous crowd urged them onward, and they brayed and groaned as they made renewed efforts to wheel the cart into the presence of King Janaka.

At last it was achieved. A priest stepped solemnly forward and opened the large iron box containing the sacred bow. Then he bid the men who had pulled the cart to assist him, and together, with the greatest of labor, they lifted a mysterious object from the box, placing it on the floor in the center of the crowded chamber.

When the men drew back and the priest removed the ornate covering from the object, the people murmured with awe and expectation.

Now the drums were still. Now the processions abruptly halted. And silence filled the great chamber.

Laksmana and Rama leaned forward anxiously. They

peered at the floor, but where they should have been able to see a marvelous bow, they could see nothing. People crowded expectantly around them, leaving only a small and empty circle in the center of the chamber. But in that circle, at the feet of King Janaka, there was nothing to be seen. Nothing. For the mighty Tiger Bow was invisible.

In the silence King Janaka joined his palms in a reverent gesture. Then he softly murmured to Laksmana and Rama, "Here is the great task that has defeated all the greatest heroes of all the lands. Here is the Tiger Bow, the object of veneration of a line of kings and princes so ancient that it reaches back into the time that existed before time began. Here is the axis of the world that all have revered but none have conquered. How, then, my young friends, can mortals know the means by which to lift and to bend this ethereal bow? If you cannot see it, how can you hope to draw the Tiger Bow and place an arrow in its powerful mouth, sending it whirling into the heavens?"

Laksmana bowed respectfully. "It is as you have said," he muttered. "How can any man conquer what he cannot see?"

From the crowd came a groan of disappointment, for the people of Janaka had come to fear that the test was so difficult that their beautiful Sita would never be wed.

"Do you then capitulate?" the little king asked in a voice full of distress. "Do you give up your chance of mastering the Tiger Bow?"

"I cannot master what cannot be seen," Laksmana murmured in shame. "I would fight the most terrible demons. I would confront and destroy your enemies. I would risk my life and my limbs to win Sita for my wife. But I cannot vanquish what I cannot hold in my hands."

Again the people murmured with disappointment and nodded in sorrow and dismay.

"And you, Rama?" the king of Janaka asked. "Do you also withdraw from the contest?"

For a long moment Rama did not answer. He glanced first at his brother, Laksmana, who hung his head in humiliation, and then he peered at the empty circle in which the Tiger Bow was hidden by its invisibility. He searched the floor for some small sign of the great weapon, but there was no tangible evidence of it. He searched his mind for the knowledge that would enable him to understand an object he could not see. But he could not understand something that was beyond understanding. Then he searched his heart for the power to imagine what he could neither see nor understand. And as he ventured through the endless labyrinth of his heart a delicate mist began to appear before him.

"Tell us now, Rama," King Janaka repeated, "do you withdraw from the contest?"

Just as Rama was about to concede his defeat, the mist completely enveloped him, rippling upward from the stones of the floor and filling the empty circle in the center of the royal chamber with a pale green illumination.

In that frail light Rama could faintly see the outline of the marvelous weapon. He could not see the bow itself, but what he could clearly see was the misty space that defined it.

Without a word, Rama stepped forward with great dignity and calm. The onlookers held their breath as they watched the young prince slowly bend toward something that only he could see.

Without hesitation, Rama lifted the Tiger Bow, which instantly became visible at the touch of his hand.

The people were so astonished that they gaped in wonder at the young hero, but they did not make a sound.

Now Rama brought the bow to his chest in a tender gesture like an embrace. As he felt the bow resting against his body, he was filled with great love and longing. Then, with a sigh, he tugged hard on the taut string, and, as Laksmana cried out in jubilation for his brother's miraculous achievement, Rama shot an arrow into the air with such speed and force that it pierced the invincible wall of the palace and streamed like a comet out beyond the world and farther still, until it took its place beside the great blazing sun and the multitude of stars.

Seven

BRIGHTLY CLAD HERALDS, wearing garlands of rosemary and mimosa, rode through the countryside on elephants painted blue and white, carrying King Janaka's proclamation to every village and town.

"Now hear me, all you good people of our land who were awakened by the roar of the string of the Tiger Bow that snapped so thunderously it reverberated every-where like thunder! Hear me! Hear me! Let it be known by all the world that King Janaka invites every creature and being of his domain to the wedding of Sita and Prince Rama of Dasaratha!"

A shout of joy went up from the villages and the rivers and the deepest jungle. Soon the pathways and roads to the palace were swarming with King Janaka's subjects. Great lords and humble peasants. Creatures that walked on two legs and creatures that walked on four legs. Dwarfs and warlocks. Enchantresses and magicians. Shadow beings and shining specters. Serpents and sun bears. Clouded leopards and herds of bantengs with the bodies of cattle and the horned heads of men. Flocks of moths and butterflies fluttering overhead among ten thousand radiantly colored birds. And in the trees, mobs of chattering apes from the Valley of the Monkeys. All responding to the call. Every creature of the sea and air and earth traveled the roads leading to the palace of King Janaka.

Horses trotted majestically, some ridden by naked brown women with wild hair and wilder eyes. Ox-drawn carriages and horse-drawn chariots rumbled over the royal roads, carrying hermits, holy men, and heroes. Sauntering battalions of elephants bearing streamers and flags, their sturdy foreheads adorned with bejeweled plates of gold and silver, lumbered toward the palace to the sound of trumpets and gongs and drums.

The noonday sun glistened and rebounded among a multitude of white satin umbrellas carried on long poles by throngs of jubilant revelers. Voluptuous women with wide hips and generous breasts, clad in diaphanous draperies, straddled water buffalo, their necklaces sway-ing with each step taken by the brawny beasts. They were flanked by muscular sentries on sleek ponies. Camels bearing towering cargoes of wedding gifts and tributes delicately threaded through the massive crowd, pausing only long enough to nibble at the bitter leaves of the margosa trees.

Amidst clouds of incense and a deluge of falling petals

and confetti, this enormous congregation finally assembled in the spacious courtyard of the palace of King Janaka, milling about jubilantly, gossiping and laughing and dancing among the chanting priests, the solemn hermits, and the bellowing vendors.

When the two kings, Janaka and Dasaratha, emerged from the massive doors of the palace terrace, perched high above the swarming courtyard, the crowd cheered in one vast voice, with trumpets blasting and drums roaring. King Dasaratha gleamed in the sunlight, so elegant and rich was his attire; while little King Janaka's smile caught an even brighter light, though he was dressed in rags and for a crown he wore only a wreath of violets and lady's-mantle.

Then through the doorway came Rama's mother, Queen Kowsalya, looking youthful and exuberant, graciously holding out her arms to the cheering crowd. Now Rama's brother, Laksmana, followed after her, handsome and strong, supporting his mother's arm as she descended the two thousand steps leading from the palace gates into the royal terrace, where priests chanted hymns and sprinkled the ground with holy water from the golden urns.

A deafening bellow arose from the throng when, at last, Prince Rama emerged into the sunlight, standing gleaming and glorious in the grand doorway of the palace and greeting the crowd with a triumphant gesture as he raised the magnificent Tiger Bow high above his head. Then he bowed reverently and quickly joined his family on the terrace, where the priests were waiting to perform the wedding ceremony at an auspicious sign from the heavens.

As they waited, the clamor of the congregation grew louder and louder, so great was the delight and expectation of every person and creature of the land and the sea. Then a cloud slowly arose from the east, rising into the sunlit sky until it opened like a billowing white flower and covered the sun. At once a marvelous fragrance swept the entire assembly, and a fragile green mist began to fill the courtyard.

As if a sign had been given, the crowd suddenly fell silent. There was a momentary wisp of cool rain, falling like a blessing, drizzling down upon the assembly.

Lightning. A colossal bolt exploding high above their heads, bursting in a white explosion at the palace's mighty portals.

Then silence and a sweet song, ringing out from the rocks and the roots of the world.

When the people and the creatures in the courtyard looked up into the smoke that billowed about the palace gates, they saw Sita emerge from the mist, standing like a goddess in the midst of the ever-obedient shadows that followed after her.

Silence.

Nothing but silence and the song of the rocks and the roots.

As Sita drifted down the steep descent of the stairway, the moon rose into the morning sky, gliding through a trail of clouds that surrounded it like a luminous wedding gown.

The stars awakened and came out, coaxing comets and meteors and one million fireflies into the heavens.

The sun closed its radiant eyes in deference to the lovely Sita, as she came hesitantly into the light. Green. Everywhere the world was green and glowing around the mysterious goddess. Her marvelous body, slender and strong. The tresses of her voluptuous green hair, reaching to her supple hips. Her bare feet, hardly touching the ground as she walked. And in her eyes, the long lean memories of the millennia.

For a moment she paused and saluted the sun. Then, with a simple gesture of her hand, she transformed the sunlight into a deep purple cushion of velvet, in which the silver moon reclined in amorous delight.

The huge assembly sighed in wonderment as the moon and sun were wed.

King Dasaratha and Queen Kowsalya gasped when the miraculous Sita took her place beside them. They peered at her, mystified by the strange power of the silent young woman who was to become the bride of their son. But Laksmana stepped forward with ease and greeted her with a deep bow, touching his fingers to his heart.

All this while, Rama's gaze had not for an instant left

Sita, so great was his love for her. And when she stood beside him and slowly, very slowly turned her superb face toward him, he was bewildered and awed by her extraordinary beauty and by the unfathomable messages that streamed from the spellbinding gaze of her silver eyes.

Bowing to his bride, Rama placed a bejeweled bracelet upon her narrow wrist. Then King Janaka stepped forward as the chimes shimmered and the gongs rumbled.

Then silence again. Nothing but silence and the song of the rocks and the roots.

"Here," the little king murmured, glancing rather sadly at Rama, ". . . here is my precious child. I cannot give her to you, for she is not mine or any other man's to give. She comes to your wedding chamber of her own choice. Freely and without persuasion. And she comes to you because she finds in you what she cannot find in herself. And so it is, and so it will be."

Now tears came into the eyes of the little king, and he turned away and sighed.

Then he gazed at lovely Sita, who stood as still and silent as a statue of ivory and jade, while the sun and the moon slowly merged in the sky.

"When she takes your hand," King Janaka whispered, "then she will no longer live at my side. When she embraces you, she will no longer brighten my days with her verdant laughter and miraculous smiles. No more will she summon the green mists of Janaka's evenings or the fragile blossoms of our springtimes. No more the tender roots of the harvest. No more will she sing the sweet songs of the earth. When she is your wife, she will be mortal and frail. Goddess no more. So it is with love, and so it must be forevermore. She will find herself in humankind, and in loving you she will lose her divinity. And so it has always been with the beings born of the eternal river."

Now King Janaka sprinkled Sita with sacred water.

Celestial gongs rang out, and from the sky came a great rain of rose petals and glittering stardust.

Carefully Rama reached for Sita's motionless hand. He did not take his eyes from her as he gently grasped her vibrant fingers.

When he touched her, a look of astonishment came over Sita's majestic and solemn features, as if she had been awakened from a long and tranquil dream.

"Now it is done," King Janaka murmured.

From Sita's mouth came a luminous gust of brilliant light. Her ever-obedient shadows suddenly dissolved. The silver in her eyes vanished. Her long hair was lifted by a breeze and its color gradually changed, turning darker and darker until it was densely black and shiny.

Then she shook her head like a swimmer emerging from a deep pool, and speaking in her newly found voice, she asked: "Who is this man? And why is he gazing at me?"

"I am Rama," the prince whispered. "And I am your husband."

And then, for the first time, Sita gently smiled.

Eight

FOR MANY YEARS, there had not been a single mirror in the palace of King Dasaratha. Only the young queen Kekay-yee possessed a looking glass, which was hidden from sight in her bath chamber. But nowhere else in Dasaratha was there a mirror.

The elderly queen Kowsalya was so tormented by the advance of age and its effect upon her features that she banished all looking glasses from her presence. Now, however, with her return from the magic kingdom of Janaka, the royal chambers were covered with mirrored surfaces in which the queen could admire her restored youth. She would hum with delight, confident that she would win back the attentions of her husband.

As for King Dasaratha, during all the long years that the queen had abhorred mirrors, he had not once studied his image in a looking glass. Great was his surprise when he now looked into the glass. There he found an old man with wrinkles and slouched shoulders and white hair. So troubling was this sudden discovery of his old age that he clutched his heart, fearful that he might die at any moment.

The king brooded alone in his chamber, timidly hiding himself from the view of his young wife, Kekay-yee, in fear that she would suddenly see him as he had only recently seen himself in the glass.

Surely his young wife no longer approved of him. Ever since his return to the palace from Janaka, he had been deeply disturbed by Kekay-yee's indifference to him. She showed no pleasure in greeting him, and refused to embrace him or to welcome Rama and Sita as her kinfolk. Instead, she turned her back on them and withdrew to her private chambers.

Now nothing seemed to please her.

When she noticed the transformation of the old queen into a vibrant young woman, her eyes filled with scorn and suspicion. And when the king presented her with the precious shaft of wheat given to him by King Janaka, she disdained the miraculous gift. She held it in her hand only briefly. The magic of the sacred wheat hissed and sputtered in her grip, sending a surge of enchantment through her limbs and taking possession of her face so that something strange and evil began to appear beneath the beauty of her masklike features. Suddenly, with a shout of displeasure, the young queen tossed the magic wheat to the floor, backing away from it in dread.

Now alone and forlorn in his lavish chambers, King Dasaratha paced back and forth all day and night, filled with irreconcilable melancholy. When he looked at his hands, he saw the wrinkled and spotted hands of a doting old man. When he looked at his belly, he saw the bulbous belly of an old fool who had pampered himself with too much food and wine. Never before had he seen himself as such a ruin of a man.

"What is to be done?" he whimpered to himself as he paced among the treasures of his palace. In every surface of every shining vase and trinket, he could see the ponderous image of time upon his face. There was no escaping his old age.

"The battlefield scorns infirmity and age," he muttered to himself.

Still he wandered through the corridors of his palace.

"A throne ever beckons the young and the strong. It is no place for an old man," King Dasaratha conceded sadly. "I must cease while my renown still shines brightly . . . before it is extinguished by age and oblivion."

And so it was that the elderly king made the difficult decision to pass his reign to one of his sons without delay. And though the hour was late, Dasaratha summoned Laksmana and Rama to his chamber.

When his sons hurried to him, fearful that his news would be of some great misfortune or impending disaster, they were relieved to find their father genial and serene. He greeted them with a warm embrace. And then he bid them to be seated.

"It is time," King Dasaratha said without hesitation or regret. "Tomorrow, one of you will be crowned as my successor."

Laksmana and Rama were astounded.

Without taking note of their response, the old king said with great simplicity and sincerity: "So tell me, which of you will be king?"

After a long silence, Rama murmured, "But father . . ."

"Which will it be?" King Dasaratha repeated in a decisive tone.

Laksmana was deeply agitated, anxiously glancing at his father. "If it must be so," he exclaimed, "then surely Rama should be your successor!"

Before Rama could object, the king sighed tranquilly. "Then it is decided. Laksmana, you are a loving son and a faithful brother. You have made a wise decision on behalf of our kingdom."

But the king's resolve did not cheer the brothers, who sat in a forlorn state, uncertain of what to say and unable to look at each other.

"You are good men," Dasaratha reassured them in a whisper. "I knew I had no cause to fear my decision. How proud you make me! Many sons would be rivals and adversaries, bringing tragedy instead of credit to their father's legacy. But Laksmana is your greatest advocate," he told Rama. "He will always stand behind you. Still, I am seized with misgivings. My mind is greatly troubled. I have terrible premonitions. I dream of comets, and I see demons in the firelight at dusk. Something ghastly is in the offing. So, dear Rama, you must be crowned without delay lest something dreadful befalls us!"

Again the father embraced his sons, and then they embraced each other.

Laksmana gazed with great admiration and devotion at Rama. "You will make a fine king," he murmured. "That much I know for certain."

"And you are a fine brother; that too I know for certain," Rama said with an affectionate smile.

Now King Dasaratha dismissed his sons.

"The night is turning to day, though we have had little rest. Nonetheless, when the sun arises, I shall call my ministers and inform them of this great decision. But my sons, until then, I beg of you, say nothing to anyone, lest some horrid demon overhear our secret before it becomes law!"

The brothers vowed to remain silent. And then they bid their father good night, and hurried away.

Shadows moved through the corridors of the great palace of King Dasaratha. Whispers shimmered like vapor in the darkness. In the distance there came the cry of a night bird crushed in the jaws of a jackal. The stars turned their heads away from the sight of the slain creature and would not shine. The moon sang her fierce and frosty songs as a sudden chill froze the delicate wings of the hummingbird. And in the sacred groves the luscious fruits of the eternal trees turned bitter and foul.

Night without honey.

Night without serenity.

Laksmana climbed into his solitary bed, unaware of the wickedness that stole silently through the night. Innocently he stared up into the darkness, overcome with delight for his brother's majestic destiny.

Rama quietly approached his wedding bed, moving through the fragrant green mist that welled up all around him and lying peacefully beside his glorious bride, who sleepily opened her eyes and smiled as she embraced Rama. Now he was so entranced by the bliss of his wife's arms that he did not sense the long claws of a demon that longed for the lives of the noble sons of Dasaratha.

Silence. The palace was fearfully still.

But already the evil had begun to take possession of the world. Even before the moon's songs were done. Before the ferocious dancing of the sun churned the dark wide horizon into a soft explosion of bronze and crimson. Already the evil had begun.

Kooni, the hunchback servant of the young queen Kekay-yee, grunted dismally as she raised the bamboo blinds of her mistress's chamber. She squinted into the dawn through milky eyes obscured by cataracts.

The queen stirred but would not awaken, despite the

growing brightness of the morning and the distant din of people in the courtyard below.

When Kooni peered down into the immense plaza of the palace, she frowned and muttered with suspicion. The capital was being decorated with garlands of lotuses, and the streets were being sprinkled with holy water. Banners and standards flapped from the roofs of the houses. Gradually the pathways and roads leading into the city were filling with people. The doors of the temples stood open, and as the sun rose, every kind of musical instrument could be heard.

Without delay, Kooni rushed through her mistress's chamber and out into the corridors, in search of an explanation for the merrymaking. When she encountered Rama's servant, who was dressed in festive white apparel, she was filled with misgivings.

"Why such a din? Why the revelry?" Kooni exclaimed disapprovingly. "All the commotion in the streets will surely vex my mistress and she will be furious."

"Have you not heard?" Rama's servant joyfully cried. "The entire palace can talk of nothing else!"

"Enough of your nonsense. Tell me at once, what is happening?"

"This very day," Rama's servant explained, "King Dasaratha has proclaimed that Rama will be installed as the heir to the kingdom!"

With a shout of alarm, the servant of the young queen rushed away, dashing into her mistress's bedchamber.

Transformed by fury, she cried out: "Awake! Awake at once, my lady! A moment more sleep and your future will be lost!"

Without opening her eyes, Kekay-yee angrily shouted, "Why are you disturbing me? Away with you! If you are not silent, I shall have you whipped!"

"Better to be whipped than to see my precious lady ruined by Rama's cunning and deceit!" retorted Kooni.

Her servant's remark brought the young queen to her feet. As she quickly drew her silken robes about her shoulders, she leaned close to Kooni and muttered in a voice full of irritation: "What is it? Has Kowsalya been whispering in my husband's ear? I knew there would be mischief. When I saw her restored youth, I knew she would plot against me!"

"But there is more," whispered Kooni. "Rama too has betrayed you!"

"Ah!" shouted Kekay-yee. "It is Sita! That monster he took for a wife! With her at his side, I knew Rama would try to do me harm. Tell me at once, what are my enemies plotting?"

"Your downfall!" Kooni hissed.

The young queen laughed.

"What harm can be done to me?" she insisted. "Rama's father is king and I am the king's favorite!"

"But today you have become the favorite of the man who is no longer king. For Dasaratha plans to install Rama on the throne this very day!"

Kekay-yee howled with unbridled fury. Her bulging eyes flashed with malice, and she whirled around, overwhelmed by frustration and wrath. She tore at her long hair, and then she struck out in blind brutality, landing a powerful blow on her servant's face.

"Curse you!" she screeched. "I will have you put to death for bringing such news!"

Kooni knelt at her lady's feet, trembling with fear. "I meant only to save you," she murmured.

"And none too soon!" the young queen barked. "So stop whimpering, and help me to dress. Quickly! Quickly! Bring me my most beautiful draperies! I must go to King Dasaratha at once!"

"But my lady, what can be done? The coronation is almost begun. The king is resolute. And Rama is loved by all the people of the kingdom! What can you say? What can you do?"

The young queen smiled a terrible smile as she placed her hands lovingly on her breasts and looked with overwhelming arrogance at her nakedness in the glass. For a moment she was silent. And then she whispered in a voice full of treachery and deceit: "I will tell you what I shall do. I shall lie. And with that lie I will bring the coronation to an end and I will also send Rama to his ruin!"

Nine

WHEN THE YOUNG QUEEN Kekay-yee swept through the halls of the palace, followed closely by her malevolent shadow, the ever-present Kooni, so furious was her countenance that the servants and nobles hurried out of her path. But as she approached the chamber of her husband, her demonic face remarkably changed into an expression of childish sweetness.

She nodded respectfully to the guards standing vigilantly at the royal door, but when she was announced, King Dasaratha was reluctant to see her.

"Not now . . . not now," he sputtered, trying to stand still while a cluster of fastidious attendants were dressing him in magnificent royal robes befitting the coronation. "Announce that I am unwell. Yes, that is it, tell her that I have an infirmity. Better yet, say that I am taking a much-needed rest."

In the midst of the king's befuddled commands, the

queen waved the guards aside and barged into his chamber uninvited.

"Did you say a rest, my lord? You are very lavishly dressed for a nap," she said with a cunning smile. "Perhaps King Dasaratha expects to have an opulent dream while he naps. About a great festivity . . . like a coronation."

"Nothing of the sort . . . nothing of the sort," the king mumbled self-consciously.

"How happy I am to hear it." Kekay-yee laughed with bitter sarcasm, kissing the old man's cheek with a disdainful expression in her eyes, though her face was fixed in a bright and innocent smile. Then, as she seated herself at the king's dressing table, the young queen added, "But perhaps I am interrupting my lord's morning repose."

With clumsy, fluttering hands, the king dismissed his entourage, turning hesitantly to face Kekay-yee. "No . . . no, my dear. It is nothing but a fitting for a new robe to celebrate my coming home to you," he mumbled. "I am quite finished with the tailors. So now you have my full attention."

"Then let us go directly to the point," Kekay-yee said in an irate voice that belied her placid expression.

"Indeed . . . indeed, to the point, my dear."

Then there was a long silence as the young queen peered intently at her husband, who was fidgeting absently with the elegant objects on his vanity table.

"If you recall, my lord, when you begged for my hand in marriage, I refused you," Kekay-yee murmured. "But you refused to accept my refusal. It was said in the courts of all the kingdoms that King Dasaratha was far too old to be my husband."

The words stung. Overcome by humiliation and indignation, the king looked away, walking slowly to one of the great windows of the royal chamber, where the morning had suddenly turned dark and dismal.

"Correct me, my lord, if I am mistaken," Queen Kekay-yee declared without a trace of expression. "But it is said by all the nobles of your court of Dasaratha that the old king was so intoxicated by the beauty and youth of Kekay-yee that he was prepared to promise anything to have her as his bride. And so, if you recall, my lord, King Dasaratha made two vows. The first vow was to make my son the heir to the throne of Dasaratha. This the priests know. This the nobles also know. And this you yourself know to be the solemn word you gave in order to marry me!"

"But I am old," the king muttered in shame, "and there has been no child."

"True enough, my lord. That was true until this very morning when I joyously awoke and felt the stirring of a new life within me!"

"How can it be?"

"Perhaps it is a gift of sorcery from King Janaka. You tell me that he has great magic and has given you many blessings since Sita came to our court. Could it be, my lord, that the kindly king has also blessed us with the miracle of an heir?"

The king was dumbfounded. "Are you quite certain?" he asked, dubiously glancing at his crafty young queen.

"Call Kooni, my servant and friend since childhood!" she exclaimed with open indignation. "If you doubt me, my lord, Kooni will confirm that I tell the truth, for she attends my every need."

"Then it is true . . ." King Dasaratha shook his head in dismay and confusion. "What a dilemma. Whatever shall we do?"

Kekay-yee answered without hesitation. "Keep your vow, my lord. Call off this secret coronation you tried to achieve while I slept! For shame, my lord. To have tried to deceive your pregnant wife. For shame!"

"Whatever shall I do?" the king repeated as the skies continued to darken.

Again, Kekay-yee answered without hesitation.

"Keep your sacred vow by announcing that you are yielding the throne to Queen Kekay-yee, who will govern until our child is grown."

Hearing these words from Kekay-yee, the old king was stupefied by pain and distress.

"Surely not! You cannot mean what you say!" he protested angrily. "You cannot expect me to betray my dear son Rama!"

And then he fell deathly silent, trying to catch his

breath and covering his eyes so he would not have to look upon the smirking face of his treacherous wife.

"Am I asleep and dreaming? Is this some demon who takes away my sanity?" the old king murmured to himself, cringing from Kekay-yee and seeking the comfort of his couch, where he collapsed in misery. He covered his ears and tried not to listen to Kekay-yee's words, but she spoke in a thunderous voice, saying the words he hoped never to hear.

"Send a messenger at once!" she shouted. "Send word to Prince Rama to put aside his coronation robes and his arrogant aspirations. Prince he may be, but never king!"

"You are that demon! You are the fiend that robs me of my delight and reason," King Dasaratha muttered with his eyes tightly closed. "You burn with evil! Now I can see you even in the darkness of my mind, and I curse what I see!"

"If you must curse someone, curse yourself for conspiring to break your vows. For plotting against me with secret plans to crown Rama! And curse your wife Kowsalya, who tempted you to favor her son Rama, while you deceived me! Go back to her and enjoy her company! I will not ask you to my chamber again!"

"Will you deny me everything?" the king moaned. "Will you deprive me of the joy of seeing Rama crowned? Will you refuse me my place beside you?" he cried, reaching out to her.

"Keep your vows!" the queen bellowed as her face was transformed by a hideous grimace.

King Dasaratha staggered from his couch, stumbling toward the demon who was his wife, only to have her turn from him. Helplessly he withdrew into the farthest corner of the chamber, surrounded by darkness, a captive of her demands, a prisoner of his vows.

Now a terrible gloom overtook him. His senses were bewildered and his features were distorted. Groaning, he felt nothing but misery and horror for the young woman whose false beauty had enslaved him. He faltered toward the queen and fell down before her. But she stepped back disdainfully, so he could not even touch her feet.

Finally he groaned, "I consent. . . . You have won and Rama has lost. Say no more. I consent."

Kekay-yee glowered with intense pleasure. Then, after a long silence, in which only the king's sobbing could be heard, she said softly, "But my lord, you forget that you gave me not one but *two* vows."

"What are you saying?"

"You also vowed to grant me any wish I might make."

King Dasaratha quivered with anxiety. In a small and strained voice, he whimpered, "And what wish is that? What more do you want of me?"

"My wish is for the safety of my unborn child," she muttered darkly, gazing intently at the hapless king. "So this is what I wish. Rama must be banished!" she exclaimed, an expression of unspeakable spite filling her face. "No harm must come to my child. You must send Rama into exile lest he harm us. You must send him far away to protect me from his hateful avarice. For my child and I will never be safe from him, knowing that I alone have forever deprived him of the power of the throne!"

The old king clutched his chest as if he might perish, so great was the pain that his young queen's words brought to him. His eyes filled with foreboding and with a million regrets for his foolish love for her. Could this demon be the beautiful young woman he had wooed and wed? If she ever loved him, surely she would bend to his pleas for compassion. But even before he could reach out in a desperate gesture to her, she turned and darted from his chamber.

Now the world darkened with grief. Now the rain would not fall. Now the flowers would not blossom. High in the dimming sky, the great eagle called Garuda swept upward into the stars with a howl of anguish. And from the depths of the deepest jungle came the long and distant wails of the great white monkey Hanuman, master of the wind. The far-flung creatures of the world cried bitterly, and everywhere there was the sound of weeping.

Ten

WHEN THE EXILED RAMA emerged from the palace of Dasaratha, a throng of anxious nobles, priests, and peasants followed after him, miserable to see their beloved prince cast out of the land of his birth. In the clouds of incense that rose from their innumerable offerings, a long lament went up, uttered by every being of the kingdom, so great was the sorrow for Rama's calamity.

Countless pleas rang out from the distraught crowd.

"Do not leave us!"

"Where will you go?"

"What will you do?"

"Will you not resist your father's command?"

"Will you not be our king?"

In Rama's splendid eyes shone a serene resignation. He calmly gazed at the countless faces that looked upon him with melancholy and disillusionment. Then he pressed his palms together in a humble gesture of farewell, and he said, "Do not grieve for me. I cherish my exile. For the sages have said that only those who venture beyond their expectations can hope to discover the unexpected."

"But must you leave us?"

"Dare you live beyond the sanctuary of our city?"

Again Rama gazed at the gentle people surrounding him.

"Do not be afraid! Look beyond the gates!" he exclaimed with an ecstatic cry. "Look out into the world beyond the world! Look with valor upon the dark places that fill you with dread and foreboding!"

"But you will surely die in the untamed world!"

"Terrible demons lurk behind every rock and tree!"

"Beyond the gates there is only death. Here alone is there safety!"

Rama held up his hand in a gesture of consecration, and then he said, "For those who fear the unknown, our city's gates are powerful guardians. You believe they stand against loathsome things that we have not yet seen or named. But my friends, those same gates can become walls that keep you from your destinies! You are afraid to open the gates. But for me those massive doors of our city are not barricades against death and suffering. For me they are doorways into other worlds!"

The people slowly turned and peered with uncertainty at the huge gateway of the city, beyond which they could only see fearsome things. Death and darkness. Things without shape or form.

"We beg you! Do not go!"

"Good fortune alone brought you back to us from the strange land of Janaka. But to venture again into the wasteland will bring only doom!"

"You will perish in the ferocious realm that lies beyond our city!"

Rama smiled innocently and nodded at his followers.

"Perhaps," he murmured, "by going where you fear to go, I shall find something precious and unknown to us. Each step of an adventurous life is a trespass. Some go willingly, while others are cast into exile. But like a swimmer, I shall ride upon the crest of adversity so I am not crushed under it. And perhaps in that dark affliction I shall find the mysterious fire that makes the shadows!"

A long moan of sorrow arose from the people as Rama arrived at the city's gates. Now he turned to leave his people. But before the signal was given to open the way to the outer world, Rama's mother, Queen Kowsalya, rushed sobbing to her son. She was crushed by the agony of seeing her princely son in rags, cast out of Dasaratha like an infidel.

"What offense deserves such punishment? To be so dishonored by your own father?" she cried out as tears flowed upon her cheeks. "What kind of father is this who sends his eldest son to death? Do not go, my son! I will go to him and plead for his clemency!"

Rama gently lifted his mother and embraced her fervently as he rocked her in his arms.

"My father is renowned for the steadfastness of his word," he murmured. "He has decided that I must leave this land, and so I go without complaint. Do not let your sweet spirit grieve, for your grief will only make this sad day more sorrowful."

"I cannot hide my grief, and I cannot conceal my defiance of your father's decree," the queen sobbed. "Yet I cannot ask you to disobey him. So, dearest Rama, let me share your exile! I cannot live here without you! Already my rival Kekay-yee pierces my heart with her every glance! What great calamity will befall me when you are gone? I beg you, let me go where you go!"

Rama kissed his mother and looked with great affection into her anxious eyes.

"My father needs you to comfort him," Rama whispered as he helped his mother to her feet. "When he realizes what he has done, his grief will be greater than ours. Now he lives in the dream of Kekay-yee's wintry enchantment. But when he awakens, he will need you to warm his embittered spirit. So I must go alone."

With a nod of resignation, Kowsalya realized that Rama's resolve could not be shaken. She feebly grasped his hands and peered up at him with intense entreaty.

"If you must go, there is one thing I ask," she pleaded. "Let your brother, Laksmana, go with you! This I beg of you, my dear son. If you will grant me only one wish, then grant me that you will go together with your brother, who cherishes and adores you above all men.

He will stay at your side and fight every evil that lies in your path!"

No sooner had the queen spoken than Laksmana emerged from the crowd and grasped his brother's hand with great affection and camaraderie.

"If you are not the king of Dasaratha," Laksmana shouted in a voice so powerful that all the world could hear, "then I will not be its prince! Open wide the gates! Together we will venture beyond this city, under the gaze of the weakness-despising stars! They will not scorn Rama and Laksmana!"

These heroic words roused the population from its melancholy, and suddenly a fervent cheer went up. Then, just as suddenly, the multitude fell silent. They turned in wonder as they reverently moved aside, murmuring in awe-filled whispers as they opened a path for a small, slender figure that drifted toward Rama.

It was Sita.

Rama's composure instantly vanished and, for the first time since his father banished him, his noble eyes filled with tears. He could not looked upon his beloved wife, dressed not in finery but in a humble robe made of spun bark, with only Rama's bracelet adorning her wrist. He had been ready to accept his sad parting with his mother and brother, but he could not bear the thought of saying farewell to his marvelous bride.

"What widow's weeds are these?" Rama muttered in distress, overwhelmed by so great a change in Sita's appearance. "I wish to remember you as the beautiful woman you were when we were married, not as a widow in the robes of mourning."

Sita embraced her husband and smiled up into his face.

"But these are not the clothes of mourning, dear Rama. They are the garments I shall wear in the forest."

"What is this?" Rama exclaimed with confusion.

With great simplicity she said, "I am coming with you."

Rama could see the determination in Sita's mysterious eyes, but still he made every effort to dissuade her from her decision to go into exile with Laksmana and him.

"My mother needs your alliance. My father needs your love," he murmured.

Sita would not heed Rama's objections. She only smiled peacefully at each of his concerns.

"There are great dangers in the jungle!"

"You forget that the jungle is my home. I know it and it knows me," Sita said quietly, embracing her husband.

"But when you became my wife you lost your powers, and you will be defenseless without them. I beg you, Sita! Stay here in safety with my mother and father!"

But Queen Kowsalya tenderly shook her head in disagreement. She could not consent to her son's departure without his wife. She hugged Sita in desperation, trembling at the thought of losing her sons and her daughter-in-law. But then she smiled tearfully, releasing Sita from her grasp and gently pushing her toward Rama.

"Go with my sons," she said in a voice full of passion. "Protect them and love them! Shine in the night. Light their dismal world. Burnish the darkness with your love. Dearest Sita . . . go with Rama!"

The Exile

And one alone will speak of being
born in pain
and he will be the wings of an extraordinary
liberty.

—Frank O'Hara

Eleven

RAMA, SITA, AND LAKSMANA disappeared into the traces of crimson that swept into the dawn sky.

As they began their long journey into exile, they passed countless stone idols guarding the way, their fierce mouths open wide, growling and showing their dreadful teeth. Then they came upon a series of hanging bridges, dangling above steep gorges and swinging in the breeze.

By now the sun blazed in the midday sky. Rama paused in the shade and looked out into the alien landscape, so unlike the friendly sights of Dasaratha that it seemed to be a different world. A different sun. A different wind. Even the birds sang songs that were unfamiliar to him. And the crickets chirped in an alien language.

Sita wandered through the green shadows, peacefully at home in this exotic land. She drank from a sparkling brook that tumbled down a cleft in a huge rock, trickling into an azure pool filled with fishes of many colors.

She splashed her face with the icy water, and as it fell back into the pool it made a marvelous sound, shimmering around Sita like a cloak of music.

As for Laksmana, he had little curiosity about his surroundings. He squatted on the ground, brooding and watchful for enemies . . . imaginary or real. Once he was satisfied that the shady resting place was safe for Sita and Rama, he sighed contentedly and became lost in thought as he honed the blade of his weapon.

Then Sita abruptly turned into the breeze, her eyes flashing and her ears quivering like a frightened deer's. Rama and Laksmana leaped to their feet, but they could not hear whatever it was that concerned Sita. And when they urged her to explain her apprehension, she hushed them and intently turned her attention to something in the distance.

Now Rama and Laksmana could hear what Sita had heard. From far away came the faint sound of snorting horses and the rumbling of their racing hooves.

Rama and Laksmana clutched their weapons as they searched the thick undergrowth for signs of intruders, caution of an attack. But when two horsemen broke through the trees, it was immediately clear that they were not enemies, but messengers from Dasaratha.

"My lords," the horsemen gasped, trying to catch their breaths as they leaped to the ground and saluted Rama and his companions, "we bring sad news. The king, your father, is dead."

Laksmana drew back in horror.

"It cannot be!" he groaned.

"It is true, my lord, your royal father is dead," repeated the horsemen. "No sooner had you left us than he paled and weakened. He wanted no physicians. He refused food. He ordered his servants to draw the draperies of his chambers, and in the dimness he cried out for Prince Rama. And then he died."

The noble brothers embraced each other in agony, and then they wept.

Sita tried to comfort them, but so great was their misery that nothing she said could relieve their sorrow.

"We must return to Dasaratha at once!" exclaimed Laksmana, brushing away his tears as his eyes blazed with anger. "Our mother is in great danger without our father to protect her! We must take the messengers' horses and leave without delay!"

The messengers fell to their knees in Laksmana's path, preventing him from taking their horses.

"What treachery is this?" Laksmana shouted, raising his spear against the men.

"We mean no treason, my lord!" the men cried. "But we must prevent you from returning to Dasaratha. Those are the orders of your mother, Queen Kowsalya!"

"If you obey her and prevent us from returning to her side, then you are dead!" bellowed Laksmana.

"If we disobey her, my lord, then we are also dead!" whimpered the messengers.

"What orders are these?" Rama demanded, grasping his brother's arm to restrain him from doing the men harm.

"The queen begs her noble sons to remain in the forest, far from Dasaratha, so they will be safe from the tyranny of young Queen Kekay-yee," one of the messengers whispered. "This is what Queen Kowsalya commanded us to tell you."

"No one is safe from Kekay-yee's ambition," the other man muttered. "No sooner was our king dead than she seized his throne and banished all his ministers, driving them out or having them murdered by her demon allies of Lanka!"

"What allies are these? How does Kekay-yee command the alliance of the demons of Lanka?" demanded Laksmana.

"We do not know how she made such an alliance, my lords. But there is no doubt that she has some sinister relationship to the terrible monster king of Lanka named Ravana!" The messenger shivered in dread.

The royal brothers trembled with anger and misgivings, peering intently at each other as they searched their minds for a solution to their predicament.

An expression of gloom filled Laksmana's face. "If Lanka is our enemy, we have reason to be vigilant," he murmured. "For there is no monster in the world more vicious than Ravana, the emperor of Lanka!"

"All you say is true," Rama agreed. "And that is all the

more reason for us to go at once to our mother's defense . . . no matter her protests!"

As the royal brothers made their way toward the horses, Sita spoke in a solemn voice.

"Think again," she urged. "Your mother's will is my will. Listen to the message she has sent. Honor her wishes. Whatever she asks, she has her reasons, and that we must do."

Laksmana ignored Sita's words, throwing up his hands in rage and shouting, "There is but one thing we must do, and that is to take vengeance upon the traitorous queen! Come, Rama, let us find this demon and her Lanka allies and kill them all!"

Again Sita spoke in a grave voice. "Hear me," she counseled. "Your weapons are useless against your grief. Bow to your tears and weep for Dasaratha. Obey your mother's wishes. Queen Kowsalya gave you life. She is the hearth of that passionate fire that burns within you. Do not consume those precious flames with vengeance and wrath. You have a far greater destiny awaiting you. Out there in the world beyond the world. Hear me. Live another day. That is your mother's will!"

Rama and Laksmana were silent.

When at last their fury cooled, they sat forlornly upon the ground with Sita, weeping bitterly.

Embracing his wife, Rama murmured, "How miserable it is to lose our father twice. Sent by him into exile only to have him die of loneliness without us."

Laksmana groaned with such futility that he trembled.

"Ah!" he stammered, "I cannot bear the disgrace! To be defeated by the barbarians of Lanka!"

The wind swept through the forest, making the trees sway and shaking their leafy heads as they towered high above the grieving brothers. Then a sweet fragrance filled the air as Sita drew back her long hair and sang a melancholy song to comfort Rama and Laksmana.

When her song was done, Rama sighed and rose to his feet, fondly touching his brother's head.

"Now let this grief and anger be done," he whispered. "And let us send word to our mother that we will do what she asks of us. Since she fears for our lives as long as the demon king Ravana lives, we will obey her wishes and remain banished far from home and homeland."

Hearing this, the horsemen instantly leaped onto their mounts, relieved to be safe from Laksmana's spear.

"That is the message we will give Queen Kowsalya!" they called out as they trotted into the underbrush. "We will tell her that you will not return to Dasaratha."

But before they were out of sight, Laksmana shouted after them, "Tell her also that we will remain in exile for only four seasons, and then we will descend upon our enemies like eagles!"

"That too we will tell her," came the voices of the horsemen as they vanished into the forest.

After somber meditation and a long rest in the cool shadows of the nut-tree grove, Rama and his companions resumed their difficult journey, going down shaded pathways lined with the wretched houses of rice farmers, whose unkempt children clustered around the strangers and peered in wonderment at their elegant faces. Then the travelers continued on their way, outward into the fields where humble workers were so numbed by their dreary labor that they were oblivious to the royal intruders. They stood in knee-deep water, bending toward the earth from morning till night as they thrust hundreds upon hundreds of rice seedlings into the rich mud.

When finally Rama and his friends approached the foothills, they entered vast groves of palms that rose on tall, lanky trunks from dense beds of luxuriant ferns. The sweet scent of the earth filled their nostrils. And everywhere were the strange songs of birds.

Now the sun became massive and red, hovering upon the horizon and turning the land amber and yellow in its long last light.

Still Rama and his companions continued on their way. Laksmana ever watchful, scrutinizing every leaf that moved. Rama deep in thought, his mind adrift in meditation. And Sita neither cautious nor solemn, but dazed by the enchantment of the opulent greenery that surrounded her with a leafy welcome. She tilted back her head and felt the spray of forest mist upon her face. Then she laughed with delight, feeling more and more joyous and free the deeper the travelers descended into the forested world. She adorned her hair with leaves and flowers. She gently touched each thing of beauty that she passed. And as she and her companions made their way into the heart of darkness, she reveled. Life flowed into her limbs. Her hair gleamed and became tinged with green. And gradually her savage power returned, deepened by her every encounter with the vibrant and untamed earth that was so precious to her.

In silence they went on. Beyond the lily ponds and the great brown river. Climbing upward among the lush rice terraces, where gleaming white herons stood majestically in the muddy water on long slender legs.

Now farther still, along perilous ridges that twisted around the haunches of the great mountain, slowly circling the rocky slopes and rising upward along treacherous goat trails that led to the misty crest.

The air became thin and blue and as fragile as a mist. The path rose abruptly, craggy and crooked, as they ascended into the fantastic moonscape called Mulu's Pinnacles; spires of sleek white stone rose high above them, creating bizarre spears of rock.

Now they labored upward, panting and breathless. Rising to the summit of the magic mountain.

94

There, at the top of the world, they could see the long valley of Dasaratha far below, with its misty temples and bejeweled palaces. An immense sense of longing and loneliness overtook them as they gazed for the last time at their homeland.

Then suddenly there was a fierce cackle.

"KAAAHHHH!"

Laksmana cried out in alarm and spun around, only to find himself facing an incredible creature perched upon the peak.

Surely, this ghastly spirit was the demon Ravana!

At once, Rama leaped in front of Sita in an effort to protect her, placing himself between his wife and the gigantic being that spread its wide wings and opened its deadly beak. At the same moment, Laksmana raised his spear with a shout that was so furious it could frighten off any monster.

But Sita only laughed at their panic, stepping calmly forward so she might speak to the great bird.

"I am called Garuda," it said in a deep voice full of pride and majesty. "Hear me. Hear me. Hear me," it cackled, opening its wings and swooping down upon the princes, where it stood towering over them. "I am not your enemy, but a comrade of your departed father, who has sent me from the land of the dead to protect his children against every evil."

"How can this be true?" Laksmana asked suspiciously, eyeing the creature with distrust.

"It is true," Garuda assured him. "Your father's spirit flies with me. So take shelter in the warmth of my wings. While I fly, follow after me in the shadow of my wide wings. I will take you safely to the river of dreams, where you may live in peace among the creatures of our magic land."

Laksmana glanced distrustfully at the great bird as he muttered his doubts to his brother.

"Will we be tricked by this flying monstrosity?"

But Sita only laughed at Laksmana's suspicions. "I know this sacred creature of the forest!" she exclaimed. "What he tells us is true. He is our friend and ally. There is nothing to fear."

Rama looked first at his wife and then at the gigantic bird. After a moment's thought, he said to his brother, "Sita is right. She is a child of the forest and knows its secrets."

"Then," Sita said with a laugh, "let us go together in the shadow of Garuda's wings!"

Now, in the approaching twilight, Rama, Laksmana, and Sita turned toward the far horizon, peering out into the world that lay beyond the mountain. From the mountain's summit they could see only the unbroken expanse of swamp forests that obscured the land, covering the world with a spacious blanket of jungle from which arose the vicious mouth of the volcano called

Anak Krakatau, roaring angrily at the sky and spewing a lofty pillar of billowing black-and-gray smoke and cinders.

Now Rama and his companions began their long descent while Garuda glided high above them.

Beyond the mountain they went, down and still farther down into the mossy silent of the forest of eternal night, where the fragile sunlight faintly beamed through the canopy of leaves far above them.

Laksmana cautiously clutched his weapon, aware of every sound, ready at any moment to defend Rama and Sita against any demon or beast. But for Sita this strange landscape was friendly and familiar. Not since leaving the lush jungle of Janaka had she felt so much at home. Here, at last, in the shadow of Garuda's wide wings, she was free and happy.

Twelve

THE RIVER OF DREAMS unfolded in the morning like a newly opened flower. Its lazy blue current was as clear and luminous as a summer's sky. Sacred trees dipped their roots into the river's mysterious depths, filling themselves with a sublime vigor, their boughs heavy with ripe and delectable fruits. The lush fields of grasses surrounding the river's edge were strewn with bright blossoms of every color. Amidst the wide green meadows were countless small pools, covered with blue and pink lotuses and fed by the warm waters of artesian springs.

Rama and Sita were enchanted with their ravishing surroundings. With each thing of beauty they encountered, they paused and reverently gazed, overcome by gratitude for the generous gifts of their newfound home.

Laksmana used his boundless energy and skill to create a fine home for them, made of colored clay walls, bamboo-lined rooms, and a broad, peaked roof of thatch. It was a wonderful dwelling, and Rama and Sita were full of praise for Laksmana when they entered their new home. They thanked him abundantly for his ingenuity, and then, without delay, they sought their sleeping chamber, for they were exhausted by the long journey to the river.

Now dusk slowly took possession of the enormous sky, and darkness descended upon the river. Silent and tranquil.

The cool and windy night curled up around the house like a cat before a fire. Its pitch-black fur glistened in the moonlight, warm and soft to the touch, until, at last, the sky began to brighten with dawn.

The morning sun was so radiant and strong that its traces slipped through cracks in the thatches of the roof and made long, luminous streaks in the dimness of the chamber where Sita dosed peacefully. Rama felt a great tenderness for his wife, gazing down at her, as sunlight danced and flickered upon her slender limbs. She seemed to be more enchanting and lovely than ever, for the river of dreams had given Rama new eyes with which to see his delightful wife. No sooner had Rama arrived on the banks of the river than quite suddenly he began to envision Sita in every beautiful thing he discovered in the water and in the fields. In every tinted sky, every flower and leaf, every bird's song he was reminded of some aspect of Sita's excellence.

Now she lay before him, languorously curled in bountiful sleep. She was a long river of life gently arching its back as it flowed endlessly through sunlit meadows.

Just as he was about to lean forward and embrace her, there came the cry of Garuda and the powerful beating of his wings, which shook the walls of the house and brought Rama to his feet.

When Rama ran out the door and into the burning sunlight, he found Laksmana already poised for battle, his weapon in hand as he searched the horizon for the enemies signaled by Garuda's cry.

But Rama and Laksmana could not see a single sign of an intruder.

Again Garuda screeched, winging his way over a dense thicket that grew at the river's edge.

Without hesitation, Rama and Laksmana rushed toward the thicket, pushing forward through the tangle of creepers and underbrush. Then they abruptly stopped and listened intently for the sounds of an invader.

They could hear nothing. The birds were silent. The crickets were silent. All they could hear was the sounds of their own breathing.

"Nothing," Rama whispered.

But Laksmana's keen eye spotted a trail. Bushes and vines had been trampled by something powerful and huge. And in the air was the foul stench of something monstrous and evil.

Followed by Rama, Laksmana cautiously searched

into the depths of the thicket, advancing with great wariness. Then he suddenly gave Rama a signal to stop and remain silent, for just beyond them, out there among the shadows of the tree trunks and dense branches, there was something truly wicked.

It was a creature so ugly that it was too hideous to be looked upon; deformed and huge, its bulging eyes sunk deep in its bony forehead, with a gaping mouth lined with glistening teeth and a large, protruding belly covered with blood.

Rama groaned at the very sight of the monster.

Laksmana made a hasty gesture to silence his brother, but it was too late.

When the demon's sharp ears heard Rama's groan, it slowly lifted its loathsome head, dropping the tattered body of the deer it was devouring. Then it grunted as it twitched its flared nostrils, wiping the gore from its lips, and peered menacingly in the direction of the royal brothers' hiding place.

Silence.

Laksmana and Rama tried not to breathe or blink an eye, so intense was the dreadful gaze of the monster as it sniffed the air and growled in a long, low, and unbearably fierce voice, its eyes fixed and glazed by the longings of an eternal and insatiable appetite for flesh.

For a moment, it seemed that the beast had not detected the presence of the brothers. But as the sun was slowly covered by a solitary cloud drifting aimlessly in the sky, the forest was cast in darkness, and in that moment the creature caught sight of Rama's vivid aura glowing in the gloom.

Suddenly it roared, rising to its bulky back legs before it charged toward them with such fury that the earth trembled beneath its pounding feet.

Then as suddenly as the beast had started, it stopped. It whined in a peculiarly feminine voice and turned its head from side to side, obliterating a lush stand of tall ferns as it lumbered uncontrollably backward and gazed in wonder at Rama's handsome face.

After a moment the monster slowly turned, and with a long, sorrowful cry it vanished into the dark forest.

Laksmana was astounded by the actions of the demon. He mumbled in confusion as he watched after the brute and slowly lowered his spear.

"If it had taken just one more step," he muttered, "you and I, dear brother, would not be alive!"

"It is true," Rama whispered incredulously, still shaken by the ferocity of the attack.

"You are a man of peace," Laksmana sternly advised, "but now you must arm yourself with your sacred bow and the arrows of fire, lest we meet this terrible monster again!"

"It will be done," Rama agreed without argument, "if only to protect Sita against this villain."

Laksmana nodded with great concern for his brother.

"Let us not be fooled by the cunning of the demons,"

he muttered as he gazed cautiously into the shadows. "There is no telling what gruesome or splendid forms they are able to assume through the workings of their evil magic!"

One evening, when Rama noticed in the woods, amidst the creepers and tall trees, a woman of the utmost beauty, he became suspicious and wary. He slowly approached her and, as he drew near, he was completely taken by her magnificent face, which was so perfect in every detail that it seemed to be an exquisite forgery of nature.

"Where are your servants and noble kinsmen?" Rama asked in a friendly voice, never taking his eyes from the woman's miraculous limbs. "For surely so great a lady could not be here alone and unattended in a forest often visited by demons."

The woman smiled lavishly and laughed, as if her laughter were answer enough to Rama's question. She lingered in the shadows of a gnarled tree, half concealing her face with a playful gesture of her hands. Rama watched her intently, wondering why she would not approach him . . . as if, perhaps, her perfection could not endure close scrutiny.

"Are you a god?" the woman asked with such simplicity that it brought a smile to Rama's comely face. "With your radiant countenance, and your eyes as large as lotus petals, and with your majestic gait and gleaming black locks crowning your head, I thought when I first saw you that perhaps you were the god of love."

For a moment, Rama was lost for words, for the woman had made this reckless and flattering statement in a tone of utter innocence, without the slightest hint of guile or deceit. Rama did not know how to respond. But the woman's amiable smile was so sincere and persuasive that it encouraged him to abandon his caution of her, and so he said, "May you be blessed for your kind words."

Again the woman laughed, creeping farther back into the shadows.

"Tell me, if you are not a god," she asked in a voice that had a trace of mockery, "then who are you and why have you come to these dangerous woods?"

"There was a king named Dasaratha," Rama told the woman, "and he was as powerful as a god. I am his eldest son, known among men as Rama. My younger brother, Laksmana, is my faithful companion. Bound by the command of our father, we have come to live in exile in this forest. That is all there is to tell."

"Then you are a mortal and not a god," she murmured with some dissatisfaction.

"Yes, mortal and guileless," Rama said flatly and without apology. "And you," he continued, carefully approaching the woman so he could see her face more plainly, "who are you? Where do you come from and what are you doing in the solitude of this holy place? Are you here without friend or family?"

"If I have no kinsman, it is by choice," the woman answered. "I abhor the ways of my people, for they are cruel and grotesque beyond belief! I came to the forest to cleanse myself of their abominations, because I wish to be different from my kinsmen."

"And what are you called?"

"I am Soorpanaka," the woman murmured in a voice tinged with malice, her eyes momentarily flashing with a crimson glow. At once she covered her face with her hand, lest Rama see the expression that had suddenly overtaken her. When she was calm again and her features reassumed their human perfection, she spoke with both pride and tenderness.

"I am the daughter of Visravas, who was the son of Pulastya. I am the sister of the lord whose very name makes the mighty gods and the most exalted emperors tremble and faint!"

With some astonishment, Rama asked, "Do you mean that you are the sister of the demon ruler of Lanka called Ravana?"

"That is who I am," she said with pride. "The princess of Lanka."

Rama was baffled by Soorpanaka's statement, for the people of Lanka were known to be anything but beautiful. He stepped closer to the woman and peered intently into her perfect face. Now, as the light brightened and he came nearer to her, he could see the magical mist that drifted ever so faintly over her alabaster skin and flawless features, concealing the reality that lurked just behind the marvelous appearance Soorpanaka had achieved through sorcery.

"If you are Ravana's sister," Rama asked with growing misgivings, "how is it possible that you appear to me as you do?"

Caught by the lust she felt for Rama, Soorpanaka could not deceive him. She approached him with a pitiable expression, tears flowing in the crimson glow of her eyes as she struggled to keep her real appearance deeply buried within the perfection of the beautiful woman's body she had assumed.

"Hear me, Rama!" she cried. "I will tell you the truth though you may denounce me for it! I can change my appearance at will. I am endowed with such great power that I can fly of my own volition! I wander in this forest, attended by my warriors and their peerless leader, Kara. By them and by all my people I am exalted. I am rich and I am mighty and I am immortal. But I would throw it all away if you would consent to be my husband and companion!"

At just that moment, Sita emerged from the house, nimbly stepping into the sunshine, her hair ornamented with bright flowers.

Seeing Sita, Soorpanaka spun around and howled as if she were possessed by a sudden rage.

"Who is this woman who comes from your house?" she bellowed.

"It is Sita," Rama said gently, "and she is my beloved wife. And so, you see, I cannot accept your gracious offer of marriage, great Soorpanaka, for it would be unthinkable for so divine a personage as you to be the miserable second wife of a mortal."

Soorpanaka glared at Sita and muttered, "How can you let this creature come near you? Can you not see what she is? Her gracious appearance is not her own! Beware! She has gained her beauty by the use of demonic magic!"

Though Soorpanaka flashed evil glances at Sita, making the very air hiss with malice, Sita came innocently forward with an expression of welcome for the handsome woman visitor.

"Look at her carefully," Soorpanaka grumbled, "and then you will see that she is not a real woman. She is a demon! You must drive her away before she does you harm!" she shouted. "Get rid of her and I will be your faithful wife!"

Rama was astounded by the fierceness of Soorpanaka's words. The notion that his wife could be anything other that what she appeared to be struck Rama as ridiculous.

With an outcry, the demon woman snatched at Sita, who recoiled from her in astonishment.

"I shall devour her while you watch!" Soorpanaka bellowed. "And then we shall live together happily without this foolish rival!"

Soorpanaka's eyes blazed like torches, and she hurled herself with a furious outcry on Sita, like a comet falling from the sky. But Rama restrained her, thrusting her back with such force that her disguise of beauty began to shatter and disintegrate.

Hearing Rama's shouts, Laksmana rushed to his brother's aid.

Now Soorpanaka made no pretense of goodwill, and suddenly her demonic spirit erupted from her in a blaze.

Laksmana dodged the scorching fire she unleashed upon him. At once, he seized his sword and with three quick thrusts he slashed off the monster's nose and ears, which fell squirming like worms to the ground.

Soorpanaka clutched her head, trying to contain herself, as the demon hidden within the beautiful woman began to burst out through her gushing wounds, spouting green blood with the force of a tempest. The demon uttered a terrible cry as the handsome flesh of the woman splattered in every direction. Rama and Laksmana were engulfed by the sickening stench of bloody slime. Then, with a revolting groan, something ghastly ruptured from the woman's disintegrating body, dripping with blood and gore. It was that same hideous monster they had seen in the woods, when Soorpanaka had first seen Rama and had been dazzled by his magnificence. A creature so ugly that Rama could not look at it. Deformed and grotesque, its bulging eyes sunk deep in its bony forehead, with a gaping mouth lined with glistening teeth, and a large, protruding belly. With a bellow of pain and rage that shook the trees, Soorpanaka flashed her teeth and showed her terrible claws before she plunged howling into the deep forest.

In a moment she was gone.

Then, miraculously, the birds began to sing.

Thirteen

FROM THE DISTANCE came the resounding clash of armor and the angry shouts of warriors. Above the canopy of the forest, a dark cloud of dust billowed upward, stirred by the marching feet of a vast army of demons as it advanced upon the house where Rama and his companions lived.

The giant eagle, Garuda, was the first to hear the clamor of the assault. Instantly the guardian bird's piercing eyes turned yellow with rage. It leaped into the air and swooped just above the treetops, screeching at the invaders. The demons shot a volley of arrows into the air, forcing Garuda higher into the sky. Again the great eagle screeched. Then it darted toward Rama's home, where it called out a shrill warning.

When Rama heard the alarm from Garuda, he seized his sacred bow and the arrows of fire.

"Guard Sita well!" he commanded his brother. "That fiend Soorpanaka returns to destroy her rival. So promise me, no matter what happens, do not leave Sita's side!"

Laksmana grasped his weapon and pressed it to his heart, shouting, "Trust me well! Soorpanaka will not harm Sita while I live!"

Then Rama quickly stretched his magic bow and hurried to meet the army of demons that advanced upon the house, crushing everything in its path. Leafy plants, gnarled bushes, delicate flowers, lush ferns. Nothing survived their tramping feet.

As Rama confronted the invaders, he instantly caught sight of the love-smitten Soorpanaka, who gazed at him with an immense longing while she hid behind the ranks of her huge army, gleefully awaiting the battle to be won so Sita could be killed and Rama could be taken as her slave.

High above Rama the eagle, Garuda, glided effortlessly in the sky, awaiting the order to attack the horde of monsters that was breaking through the pulverized forest and descending upon the clearing surrounding the house. There they stood stupid and inert, their crimson eyes flashing. An endless succession of warriors like a menacing wall of armor and glistening weapons. Grunting and snorting as they huddled around their demon commander, Kara.

Rama slung his bow across his shoulder and stood quietly before the invaders.

"What is your purpose?" he called out to Kara. "We are

the sons of Dasaratha, two brothers called Rama and Laksmana, who have come with my wife, Sita, to live in this forest in peace. Why do you seek to do us harm?"

The demon commander, Kara, flashed his grotesque smile, showing his long teeth. Then he shouted back to Rama:

"We are pledged to Princess Soorpanaka not to harm you or your wife."

"Then why are you here?" demanded Rama in a strong voice.

"To escort you across the great water to the palace of the greatest lord in the world, our master, King Ravana!"

"We will not go willingly to visit a monster like Ravana!"

"Then," Kara bellowed, raising his arms as a signal to attack, "you will go unwillingly!"

In fear for the life of her husband, Sita rushed to the door of the house, restrained by Laksmana, who would not allow her to run to Rama.

When Sita saw her husband confronted by a vast horde of demons, she screamed and raised her left hand toward the sky.

Magically, as if in response to her voice, a vast darkness fell upon the world. Black clouds ferociously tumbled into the sky, like herds of elephants gone mad, stampeding upward and outward in every direction. A shower of blood fell upon the quiet earth. And the chariot in which Kara rode lurched wildly as the earth trembled beneath its sturdy wheels.

Now the sun itself shriveled and vanished in midair as a shadowy disk enveloped it and overpowered its heavenly light, which flared and sputtered, turning into a burning halo around the dying god of daylight.

In the darkness the moon hurled herself into the heavens, sending her incantatory light into the heart of the jungle. At once, every creature, beast and bird, cried out in deafening shrieks, charmed into madness by the moonlight. The jackals crouched in the thickets and made fiendish howls. The herons and vultures raised a ghastly shriek. And the eternal fires of the temples were smothered by the powerful breath of the howling creatures that made a fierce wind.

The commander of the demons, Kara, peered fearfully into the heavens, uncertain of the meaning of the omens that appeared all around him. But after just a moment of hesitation, he slowly gave the signal, and his barbarous army moved forward against shining Rama, who stood peacefully with his arms at his sides, unwilling to fight unless his enemies first attacked him.

As Kara's demons advanced, wild beasts raced forward to bar their way, roaring at them with such ferocity that the demons glanced nervously at Kara before continuing their maneuver.

Stars as numerous as fireflies darted into the darkness.

Comets of sinister aspect fell on the earth without a sound. Silent explosions lit the sky.

Standing tall in his chariot, Kara raised an angry war cry. But suddenly his left arm twitched and withered and his voice died in his throat. His eyes filled with tears. His head throbbed. He trembled with fear. But despite all these dreadful omens, he would not turn back his army.

"I am Kara!" he shouted. "In all things I am victorious!"

The demons rallied to Kara's boast, shouting curses at Rama and rushing toward him as they loosed a thousand arrows.

Again Sita screamed and raised her hand.

Miraculously Rama received the arrows hurled against him without injury. As a sacred mountain could not be injured when struck by lightning, so Rama, when struck by countless arrows, remained steadfast and whole.

Again Sita cried out.

The heroic bird Garuda heard her cry and swept the air just above the demon warriors, severing their hideous heads with his huge and spiny beak. Again and again Garuda dived upon the invaders, trying to drive them away, trying to save Rama from their brutal attack. When the demon warriors came close to Rama, the great eagle grasped them in his powerful claws, lifting their bodies high into the sky and then dropping them to the rocky summit of the sacred mountain, where the hyenas hungrily feasted upon their broken limbs.

Again Garuda returned to the battlefield, snapping his forceful jaws at the demon commander Kara, who sped away on his chariot.

Garuda pursued him. And just as the eagle was about to clutch Kara in his terrible grasp and carry him aloft, Kara leaped high into the air as if he were a tiger. With a war cry, he swung his sword with all his strength, cutting off the bird's wide wings with two quick thrusts.

Garuda lurched in the air, screaming with pain as he twisted and reeled. For a moment he hung motionless as if the sky itself had embraced him in order to keep him from falling. Then, with a sickening whimper, Garuda plummeted toward the earth, crashing at Rama's feet.

Seeing his guardian and friend lying dead before him, Rama's eyes filled with tears, and his heart filled with rage. Now he slowly took the sacred bow into his hands and, stretching the string with all his might, he sent the arrows of fire into the air like a torrent of blazing comets. They rained down upon the demons, ripping into their flesh, which caught fire and burst with a shower of foul blood. Then the monster warriors crashed to the ground. Their bows, their banners, their shields, and their armor were strewn everywhere in bloody heaps. Struck down, disemboweled, torn and hacked into pieces, thousands of demons fell on the grisly battlefield, which was covered as far as one could see with their reeking corpses.

Seeing his great army destroyed by a single mortal,

the demon Kara was seized with rage and hurled himself on Rama. From his bow he loosed fiendish arrows that were transformed into vicious biting serpents when they struck Rama.

When Rama was wounded by the venomous snakes, Kara gave a mighty shout.

But Rama did not waver. His sublime body became a clear and smokeless flame, blazing brightly as it incinerated the wriggling serpents and healed Rama's wounds, filling him with the strength of two thousand gods.

Holding his sacred bow above the fire that raged all around him, Rama shot six arrows at one time, releasing the string of his bow with such force that it resounded like thunder.

One arrow struck Kara in the head. Two arrows pierced the demon's two arms. And the remaining three arrows punctured his chest.

But Kara's terrible wounds did not stop him for a moment. So Rama aimed again with such precision that one arrow shattered the axles of Kara's chariot and another severed Kara's bow at the exact place where he held it.

Still Kara would not admit defeat.

His bow broken, deprived of his chariot, his pride and his body injured, Kara sprang to the ground with his sword in hand and stood waiting for Rama to challenge him.

"Surrender now!" Rama called in a voice full of compassion. "No matter your heroism, you will lose this battle. For ruthlessness and cruelty can never defeat happiness! Hear me! You will fall at my hand. Though you are a great warrior you will not win, for Sita is watching over me!"

"I am sworn to my lord, the king Ravana!" Kara shouted back in defiance. "You are not my sovereign! And I will not listen to you any more than I will listen to the wind!"

With measured steps the demonic warrior advanced upon Rama, hollering, "Beware, mortal! Though I am commanded by Soorpanaka to spare your life, I will forget her orders if you thwart my purpose! I am here to take your wife for the pleasure of my king. Soorpanaka has filled his ears with tales of Sita's perfection, so I am commanded to abduct her. That is my charge, and that I will achieve though it costs me my life!"

Rama only laughed at Kara's bluster.

Filled with fury, Kara could not endure the pious expression on his adversary's handsome face. With a shout of rage, he hurled his sword at Rama. It left his hand like lightning, resounding with a thunderbolt and consuming the very air with its savage heat as it sailed toward Rama. But just as that deadly sword was about to strike Rama, the prince raised his sacred bow and shattered Kara's weapon while still in the air.

"Surrender!" Rama repeated as Kara's sword fell in fragments to the ground. "You have no warriors! You have no weapons! There is nothing left for you but surrender."

"You are bluffing!" shouted Kara. "You look upon me and are filled with the terror of your mortality." Kara growled as he continued to advance on Rama. "Despite your boasting, you are a coward!"

"You cannot kill me with insults!" Rama laughed.

"Then I must kill you with my bare hands!" Kara cried as he began to burn with terrible wrath.

His monstrous body was covered with sweat. His eyes were inflamed. Maddened by the smell of his own innards slowly oozing from the wounds in his belly, Kara rushed at Rama with a howl that shook the earth and sent the moon into hiding.

Seeing the mountainous demon approaching him in full fury, Rama skillfully stepped aside, giving himself time to place the most sacred arrow with the tip of gold against the string of his mighty bow. Then, with a long and sorrowful outcry, he let the fatal arrow loose.

It struck Kara in the eye with such force that it split open his gigantic skull. Flames burst out. A deluge of black spiders and worms spewed into the air. Then, with a pathetic whimper, the demon fell dead.

Now all that could be heard was Sita's long song of praise as the moon and sun came together into the sky.

Fourteen

RAMA LAY IN THE SHELTER of Sita's gaze.
Night lingered in the heavens, so entranced by her
beauty that it could not bear to leave the sky. The stars
also gazed down on her perfection. And the moon tenderly fingered her shimmering ebony black hair as it
sang its long song to night-blooming orchids and lilies
that sprang up at Sita's feet.

Now she sat quietly beside her husband, watching
over him as he peacefully slept. Her eyes flared green
and amber as she guarded him, fearful that the demons
might return at any moment.

But Rama was lost in the magic of the night, little
aware of his wife's powers. He snorted softly as his mind
meandered from his body and descended into the misty
land of dreams.

Sita could not sleep. But Rama was at peace. And
Laksmana serenely dozed in his own chamber, for both
of the heroic brothers felt certain that their battle with

the demons had been won. Sita, however, knew the world of demons far better than her princely husband and his courageous brother. They were creatures of the daylight. They understood all things that glittered in bright sunlight. But Sita knew the world beyond the luminous world of day. She knew the region of the heart that slept in the shadows of the jungle. In the teeming river of the night. In the time of the eclipse. And so she knew that Soorpanaka's demonic love of Rama would inevitably bring great trouble to them.

"Are you sleeping, my husband?" Sita whispered.

Rama gently moaned as he slept.

"Then listen. Listen to what I say," Sita murmured as her eyes flared and the moon danced and fluttered in her hair. "Far away in the dark, beyond the water and the shore, the demon king Ravana is dreaming. And in his dream, I am his wife and you are his slave."

For a moment Sita was silent as she watched Rama's mind slowly wafting from his gently twitching nostrils . . . rising, twisting, and spinning dreams in the air.

"Are you sleeping, my husband?" she whispered. "Then dream the dream that Ravana dreams."

Rama lazily turned in his sleep. And when he turned, he suddenly found himself in a vast chamber. Far away and beyond a nameless sea. In a strange land.

Darkness.

Then, suddenly, torches flared. The walls came alive and cowered. The very stones of the chamber were jolted by something wicked and loathsome in the air. Screams resounded from the labyrinth of corridors that spilled into the cavernous hall. Somewhere women sobbed. Wolves bayed in misery. Infants whimpered. And from high in the murky air a cascade of dead flowers and rotting leaves rained down on a ferocious figure that sat motionless upon a gigantic throne of blood and bones.

It was Lord Ravana, the king of the demons.

His ghastly eyes were closed as he slept and dreamed the dream that Rama dreamed.

All around him were once-mighty kings whom Ravana had abducted and, with his wicked magic, transformed into brutish slaves that were neither men nor beasts. These pathetic creatures anxiously watched Ravana, dreading that he might open his incendiary eyes and obliterate them with a fiery glance. Trembling and pitiable, they stood mumbling praises, while their hands were perpetually raised in adoration, lest Ravana be dissatisfied with the abundance of their devotion to him.

Hanging from every wall were the severed heads of creatures great and small, staring out at Ravana without roars or growls. Animals subdued and vanquished from their jungle. Silent trophies for the dark kingdom. Lifeless yet still living, the untamed heads dreamed of the moonlit forests from which they had been stolen.

Beautiful women, kidnapped from far-flung kingdoms, groveled in fearful submission at Ravana's side, caught under his terrible claws that lay heavily upon them like barbed and poisonous harnesses and manacles.

In the black cobwebs of a dingy corner sat a hag making a dreadful music on an instrument created from human bones and strung with human hair. Disembodied eyeballs, held captive behind the strings of the ghoulish harp, stared out in everlasting horror, blinking helplessly as they streamed with bloody tears. Along the framework of the instrument were dismembered lips, nailed fast, desperately trying to form the sound of a cry for help.

The ghastly harp recoiled and shivered in the hands of the hag. And each time her claws touched the strings there was the agonizing howl of drowning children.

Pale light in the darkness.

The god of fire had been captured by King Ravana and thrust into a cage so small that he was forced to bend low and hopelessly sputter and flicker, unable to leap into the air and lift the excruciating gloom of the chamber.

Even the god of death stood in shackled agony, chained to the wall and forced by Ravana to sound a gong as time passed endlessly.

The hollow pulse of endless time.

And nothing more.

Clouds of incense swirled in the air as Ravana snored. Then a feeble breeze rescued the perfumed smoke, which darted away from the demon's mouth, lest he take a deep breath and suck it into his abysmal lungs, where ten thousand captive birds beat their fragile wings against his ribs, imprisoned from the light.

The merest trace of incense was left hanging in mid-air. The colossal surge of the demon king's breath caught the smoke and drew it helplessly into his nose. As the incense tickled his nostrils he snorted violently, shook his gigantic head, and leaped to his feet.

Instantly his slaves, concubines, and ministers winced with foreboding, backing away from the king whose very flesh seethed with corruption and decay.

"I have had a dream!" Ravana exclaimed.

Then he glared at his sorcerers and shouted, "Tell me the meaning of my dream!"

The magicians recoiled in fear. And as they trembled, they stammered, "What dream is this, my lord?"

Ravana groaned as he lumbered among his ministers, glaring down at them.

"A light came from a stone," he stammered in a daze. "A voice came from a river. A woman. A beautiful woman. More beautiful than all my wives! How can that be?" he bellowed as he frowned at his sorcerers, awaiting their explanation. "The woman was in my dream but would not look at me! She would not adore the great lord Ravana! How can that be?"

In a fury of indignity and impatience, Ravana pounded his fist upon the massive walls, which shuddered at his touch.

"Tell me at once! What is the meaning of such a dream?" he demanded.

The magicians fumbled and stuttered, but they could not answer their king's question.

"Answer or die!" the demon king bellowed.

"Uh . . . uh . . . uh," one magician stammered in desperation. "Did this woman have a name, my lord?"

"Yes," Ravana roared, "of course she had a name! Her name was Sita!"

At these words the magicians were thrown into a complete panic. They huddled together and they whispered to one another and they anxiously glanced at their king. Then one of them fearfully approached Ravana and whispered, "If she is called Sita, my lord, then she is the wife of the mortal named Rama who is loved by your sister."

"I care nothing about my sister's obsession with this feeble mortal!"

"But . . . but . . . my lord, he is not feeble by any means," stammered another magician as his legs trembled and his breath came short. "He is the same man who slew Kara, your greatest warrior! And he is the brother of the man named Laksmana who mutilated your dear sister Soorpanaka!"

"Ah!" bellowed Ravana so loudly that the earth shook. "Then I will take revenge on all of them! Go to him and kill him!"

"But Rama is powerful, my lord! With his bow alone

he destroyed Kara's vast army. Only the foulest magic will subdue him!"

"Then call up your most vile spells and strike him down!" Ravana muttered as his eyes bulged and blazed. "First I shall take his wife"—he snickered wickedly—"and then I shall take his life and feed his body to my lovesick sister Soorpanaka!"

"But how can we accomplish what Kara and all his mighty warriors failed to accomplish, my lord?"

"Send for Mareecha!" Ravana commanded. "The rest of you be gone! For only Mareecha can do this deed. He is the most loathsome of all my magicians! Go to him in his filthy den, and tell him that I charge him to seek out this mortal called Rama. That is my order! Mareecha will find Rama. And when Mareecha finds him, he must use his most cunning magic to assume the form of a golden deer."

"Ah," chanted the gloating chorus of magicians.

"For only such a rare and handsome animal will draw Sita away from the vigil of Rama and Laksmana. And once she is unprotected by them, then, my monstrous friends, the rest of the deed I myself shall do," Lord Ravana muttered with a sickly smile.

His laughter rang out in the dark chamber. Screams resounded from the labyrinthine corridors that spilled into the cavernous hall. Somewhere a woman sobbed. Wolves bayed in misery. And from high in the murky air a cascade of cinders and flesh rained down upon the great lord Ravana, sitting motionless upon his gigantic throne.

Ravana's resounding laughter echoing everywhere.

Rama awakened with a start, the sounds of the demon's voice still ringing in his ears.

"Ah," Rama muttered with great distress, embracing his wife and staring with apprehension over her shoulder into the darkness of the forest beyond. "I have had a dream."

"And tell me, dear Rama, what did you dream?" Sita urged.

For a moment Rama was greatly confused. Then he whispered, "I am not certain, but I know that we are in great danger."

"What danger did you see in your dream?" Sita entreated as she stroked Rama's feverish brow.

"Ah," Rama sighed. "The dream is gone. Gone. Just a moment ago it was clear and vivid, but now it is gone. And all that remains is a mysterious omen of great danger!" he whispered as he glanced anxiously into the black clouds that were quickly enveloping the frail light of dawn.

Silence.

And in that silence a bird's jubilant morning song was stifled by the growl of a beast. And in the air was the stench of something foul and evil recklessly descending upon the lush green world of the sacred river.

Fifteen

JN THE COOL GREEN FOREST there was a ripple of air. Then something strange began to happen among the orchids and fig trees in the emptiness of a dank clearing. The ground fluttered like smoke. The grass rustled as if it were swept by a ghostly breeze. The sparrows closed their wings. The trees swayed and their branches hissed and bent upward. Space seemed to collapse upon itself. And then, quite suddenly, a marvelous creature took shape, shimmering in the air like a phantom, twisting wildly as shifting mists turned into a puff of silver smoke. It quivered and burned with dazzling jewels, until it gradually assumed a strange physical form.

It was a miraculous deer. Beautiful and unreal.

The points of its magnificent horns were studded with precious gems that glistened in the fragile light. Its gleaming hide was dappled. Its delicate mouth was the color of a red lotus enfolded by its ebony lips. Its long, slender ears were azure tinted. Its supple belly sapphire in tone. Its sturdy flanks the color of madhuca flowers. Its hooves emeralds. Its legs fleet of motion. And its haunches gleamed with all the hues of the rainbow.

And so it was that while Rama slept and Laksmana stood guard, the demon magician Mareecha transformed himself into a ravishing deer of iridescent colors, studded with countless jewels and golden ornaments. So handsome was this phantom creature that the whole forest was filled with murmurs of admiration for its ethereal radiance.

It roamed among the palms and karnikara trees. And eventually it approached Rama's house.

Sita was enjoying the sun as she wandered among the flowers that grew in profusion by her house. When she heard a sound, she glanced into the forest. And while she watched in delight, the phantom deer slowly came into view.

Sita was awed by the creature's beauty. So brilliant and mirrorlike were the lustrous gems and shining ornaments clinging to the miraculous deer that it cast back Sita's own reflection. In that likeness she could see herself riding astride the fantastic creature, wild and free, her long hair flaring out in threads of light.

Sita had no wish to possess anything of the world, but now, beholding the wonderful deer, she was suddenly overtaken by an intense desire to capture it.

She carefully approached it, holding out her hand.

Then she tempted the creature to come to her, offering it tender grass and bright, succulent blossoms, but the wondrous deer had no interest in such choice food.

Sita was baffled by the deer's behavior. Never in her life had an animal rebuffed her. But now, as she stealthily approached the animal, its eyes blazed. For a moment she recoiled, for it seemed to her that if this miraculous creature would not come to her, then it could not truly be a child of nature.

But the more she watched the deer the more entranced with it she became. Eventually she was so beguiled by its beauty that she continued to pursue it, moving farther and farther into the trees and the murkiness of the jungle.

All this while, Laksmana had been standing in the doorway of his house diligently watching Sita and the mysterious deer. When he noticed that she was being enticed from the safety of their home, Laksmana called out to her.

Reluctantly, she turned and returned to the compound.

"Beware of unknown things," Laksmana warned Sita as he warily watched after the fleeing creature.

Sita laughed at Laksmana's suspiciousness.

"You are too much the warrior," she admonished with a smile. "You see an enemy in everything."

"I see what I see," Laksmana muttered.

"You see what you want to see," Sita insisted.

Laksmana fell silent. He shrugged with chagrin, a wounded expression filling his face.

Noticing Laksmana's embarrassment, Sita touched him gently on the arm.

"I mean no offense, dear brother," she said softly. "For as you say, it is true that the creature is unfamiliar. But still I do not fear it."

"Fear what you do not understand," Laksmana admonished glumly.

Again Sita laughed cheerfully, embracing Laksmana.

"If you truly saw what I had seen," she exclaimed, "you too would agree that the phantom deer is wonderful!"

"A thing of evil," Laksmana muttered to himself, realizing that nothing he could say would change Sita's mind.

"What evil is this?" Rama asked, coming from the chamber where he had been sleeping. "And why does Laksmana sound so forlorn?"

"His battle with me was lost." Sita laughed while Laksmana pouted. "He would not capture a handsome creature I found in the forest."

"Evil . . . something evil," Laksmana insisted.

"But how can anything so beautiful be evil?" Sita asked innocently.

"Where is this animal you crave?" Rama asked. "Surely it is best left where it is."

Hearing this, Sita turned from her husband and her eyes filled with tears.

Rama was amazed by her distress. Embracing her, he said, "Do you love this beast so much that its absence brings tears to your eyes?"

"Never before have I seen myself," she murmured in a tone of despair. "And now I will be forever incomplete and sorrowful without that creature at my side. For when I looked upon it, what I saw was myself."

"Then you will have it!" Rama valiantly announced, fetching his sacred bow and starting toward the forest where the deer had disappeared.

Laksmana quickly followed his brother, but Rama gestured for him to stay with his wife.

"Sita must not be left unattended," he warned. "While I go in search of this animal, you will stay with her."

Reluctantly Laksmana returned to Sita's side and watched as Rama vanished into the underbrush.

With his bow held ready, Rama carefully stalked the golden deer. He was so intent upon its capture that he did not give heed to Laksmana's words of caution. All he could think of was Sita's sorrowful face and her ardent wish to have the creature.

"She shall have it," Rama murmured to himself as he pressed into the dark forest. "And then she will smile again."

When he finally spied the glittering deer, hidden among the branches, he silently moved toward it. But at that moment, the animal heard him and dashed away.

Then, as suddenly as it bolted into motion, it paused and gazed back at Rama, waiting for him to approach.

But when Rama could almost reach out and touch the miraculous deer, again it darted away, only to stop and look back at him. Again and again. As if it were tricking the hunter to venture ever deeper and deeper into the darkness of the forest.

Now the encampment was far behind Rama. He could faintly hear his wife's voice calling after him.

He had chased the deer through valleys and over mountain trails and then into the jungle world far beyond the sacred river. Rama was being drawn ever farther from Sita by a rash determination to please her.

Gradually, as the twilight overlook the land, it occurred to Rama that he was being tricked. Perhaps Laksmana had been right after all. This was no ordinary prey. But still he could not resist the lure of the forbidden beast. He rushed on and on as darkness descended. Farther and farther. Until, at last, the deer's strength began to fail and Rama's exceptional endurance allowed him to overtake it.

Now the magic deer would belong to Sita!

Just as Rama was about to throw himself upon the animal and wrestle it to the ground, something remarkable happened. Instead of helplessly succumbing to his strength, the deer suddenly roared in a monstrous voice and turned on him, drawing back its oozing jowls to reveal long, fierce teeth that could not be the teeth of a deer.

Taken completely off guard, Rama cried out in surprise.

At that moment, the grisly creature saw its opportunity, and as it hissed and as its eyes blazed, it charged Rama with such speed and force that a cloud of dust flew into the air.

Before Rama could sidestep the beast's furious assault, it savagely butted into him, knocking him to the ground. Then it fell upon him and its terrible teeth tore into Rama's shoulder.

Sita, hearing the distant echo of Rama's cry, exclaimed to Laksmana, "Ah! Something terrible has happened to my lord. Go at once and help him!"

"Even the tricks of a magic deer are no match for Rama!" Laksmana insisted, restraining Sita from running into the forest. "You must stay here with me as Rama commanded."

Sita was seized with panic. She desperately embraced Laksmana and cried, "Do not stand here while he dies! I beg you! Go! Go now! Go and save Rama before it is too late!"

Overwhelmed by Sita's fear and driven by his own confusion and anxiety, Laksmana lurched into motion, clutching his weapon and plunging into the forest.

"Rama!" he bellowed. "Where are you? What has become of you?"

Rama heard his brother's shouts, but he could not respond, so great was his battle with the demon

Mareecha, whose grotesque arms burst out of the body of the deer and savagely snatched at Rama's eyes.

Rama bellowed. Pulling himself free of Mareecha's claws, he staggered backward, trying to catch his breath as his hand automatically reached for an arrow. Without a moment's delay, he frantically aimed at the monster, and let the arrow fly just as Mareecha was making a desperate effort to flee from the deer's body and escape into the forest.

But it was too late.

Rama's arrow hissed through the air like a bolt of lightning. With a blast of explosive sound, the magic arrow plunged into the wicked magician's heart.

Mareecha froze in midair. His eyes and mouth opened wide. For a moment he was silent, and then he let out a scream of pain. He writhed and squirmed helplessly, pierced and skewered by the arrow, unable to escape, as the body of the false deer burst into flames and shattered, crumpling and sputtering, until nothing remained but the scorched limbs of the sinister magician fuming and bubbling upon the forest floor.

At just that instant, Laksmana broke through the underbrush, swinging his sword as he hurtled to Rama's defense.

With a shout, he stopped short, staring first at Rama and then peering down at the corpse of Mareecha.

It was at that moment that the two brothers understood their folly. They instantly realized that they had fallen into a trap.

"Sita!" Rama sobbed, overwhelmed by the realization that she was alone and defenseless at their distant home.

Without another word, the brothers frantically raced toward the encampment, crying out with long and harrowing shouts.

They pushed through the branches that ensnarled them. They staggered up the mountain trails and plunged through streams. They crawled through quagmires and tumbled down rocky ledges. Until, at last, they crashed through the branches and rushed toward their house.

"Sita!" Laksmana called.

But she was nowhere to be found.

"Sita!" Rama wailed.

Silence. Nothing but silence.

Darkness.

And then the muffled sound of a voice, calling out for help.

The brothers sped into the clearing behind the house, clutching their weapons.

"Sita!" Rama screamed when he saw something monstrous dragging his helpless wife by her long hair. Sita was in the clutches of something so hideous that the very sight of it made Rama ill.

"Sita!" Rama howled in misery as the monster laughed his loathsome laughter.

"Sita!" Rama moaned as the demon stepped upon his celestial chariot and raced into the night sky, hurtling in a fiery cloud toward the dark kingdom of Lanka.

"Sita! Sita!" Rama whimpered, peering hopelessly after his wife, who vanished into the unfathomable darkness beyond the moon.

The Battle

The heroes of all time have gone before us.
. . . and where we thought to find an abomination,
we shall find a god.
And where we had thought to slay another,
we shall slay ourselves.
Where we had thought to travel outward,
we will come to the center of our own existence.
And where we had thought to be alone,
we will be with all the world.

—Joseph Campbell

Sixteen

$\mathcal{E}$VERYWHERE IN THE LAND of the volcano there was ice and fire.

The cliffs and ledges were hung with long, sharp, glistening icicles. The crevices in the gray rock billowed with steam and leaping flames that shot high into the sky. Amidst the blazing gases were geysers of boiling water that erupted from the earth and showered the slopes, where the water hissed and sputtered before turning into ice.

The thin air was radiant in the burning sunlight. And endless tiers of gray clouds lay far below the freezing summit of the angry volcano.

There was no vegetation. There were no creatures. Only the sullen wind that inhabited this desolate land, far from the sacred river and farther still from Dasaratha.

Rama and Laksmana struggled across the slick ice, dodging the roaring flames and the spouts of scalding waters. Many lonely days and nights had passed since

Sita was abducted by Ravana, the demon ruler of Lanka. In those sad times, the brothers doggedly followed the fragile trail of rumors and hearsay that they hoped would lead them to Sita. But she was nowhere to be found.

"I search the sky for her," Rama murmured to himself. "But I cannot find the slightest sign of her despite all my longings. I do not know where she could have been taken. She could be in the distant sky, adrift in Ravana's airborne chariot. She could be held captive in a desolate prison full of demons. She could be buried alive in a suffocating tomb. I can only hope that somehow and somewhere there is a creature that will remember her sorry plight and will tell me where to find her!"

Now, as Rama and Laksmana began the long descent over the shoulder of the mountain, the sun moved along the distant horizon. The huge, black clouds of the rainy time rolled relentlessly into the sky. Lightning flashed, and thunder rumbled across the earth. Suddenly, with a sound like a river bursting its banks, the rain began to fall in a deluge so heavy and powerful that Rama and Laksmana were bent forward by the downpour.

The days of the great rains obscured the sky. Water tumbled endlessly from the heavens, running, rushing, splashing down the slopes, prodding huge boulders from the cliffs, sending vast mud slides gushing down the mountainside. The cuckoos and nightingales were nowhere to be seen. The orchids' fleshy petals trembled and broke in the lash of the storm. Deep within the shelter of stony recesses and dark caves the vigilant eyes of animals glowed. Life seemed to have vanished in its flight from the tempest. Only straggly creepers and vines, stirred by the abundance of moisture, ran riotously over the rocks and muddy hollows.

Rama sat upon a rock in the rain, overcome by turmoil and melancholy, for he knew that there was no hope of finding Sita during the time of the great rains.

When Laksmana urged him to join him under the shelter of an overhanging rock, Rama refused to move. He could not seek solace when he felt hopeless and sorrowful.

"While we sit here, Sita is the prisoner of a monster!" Rama moaned. "I want no comfort. I would rather stay in the rain and be as miserable as Sita."

On every day, there was something that reminded Rama of Sita. The wind in the trees reminded him of her lovely hair. The gushing floodwater reminded him of the strength in her powerful glance. When the lightning burst in the sky, Rama imagined the blistering bolts as monstrous faces grinning down on Sita as she recoiled and cried out for her husband. When he saw an occasional bird's futile attempt to fly against the rain, he imagined Sita helplessly trying to escape her captors.

Laksmana tried to cheer him, but nothing would raise his spirits.

"My life is not whole without her," Rama murmured

when Laksmana braved the storm and came to sit in the pouring rain at the side of his forlorn brother. "She is more than a wife to me," he said, looking out into the blinding downpour as his tears mixed with the rain. "She is a new moon in the night sky. She lights the darkness. She is a fire in the lightless interior of my life. I cannot find myself without her to remind me what I have been and what I am becoming. She is the dawn and the dusk. In her eyes I see new springs unfolding from old winters. I see the frail trickle from the earth that becomes the sacred river, and I see the faint embers that become the raging fires of the angry mountain. In her I see the place in the branch that imagines the leaves. In her eyes I find myself when I am afraid that I am lost. Where I am ferocious, she is subdued; and where I am feeble, she is strong. I cannot walk on the green grass without thinking of her. I cannot find my way into my dreams. I have tried, but I cannot awaken from my barbaric sleep without the sound of her voice calling to me. I do not understand why, my brother, but without her I can no longer be what it is that I am."

Laksmana gazed intently at his brother, mystified by what he said, for these were not the words of a man from the kingdom of Dasaratha. For such men, marriage was like the city walls: barriers that kept them safe from the unknown. In Dasaratha life was lived and children were born and the days were good when all the days were the same. But for Rama the days had changed and the gates had opened wide. Now Rama could hear the world beyond the world. And now Sita had become that open gate leading into the unexpected and the unknown.

"If I have lost her, then I have lost myself. Without Sita I cannot find my way."

Laksmana nodded in confusion and glanced absently into the heavens. For as Rama spoke the skies brightened and the rains ended.

The horizon gleamed with golden sunlight. On the mountain's perilous loins, lush, wide leaves unfurled in the brightness that overtook the shadows. Far below, the jasmine bloomed and the nut trees were covered with delicate white blossoms. The angry mountain's fiery roar fell silent. And Rama's mood brightened as the heavens brightened.

The brothers stood on a narrow ledge that jutted out from the volcano's slope, gazing with delight into the distance.

Far below was the Valley of the Monkeys. Even at such a distance, Rama and Laksmana could hear the song of the nightingales and the croaking of bullfrogs. Peacocks came out into the dazzling sunlight, shaking the rain from their magnificent plumage as they spread their dazzling tails.

Floodwater that had raged and roared in the time of the rain changed into lazy streams that meandered peacefully through the bogs bordering the vast jungle. And in the midst of the bogs golden clusters of dates ripened on the areca palms that stood windless and tall.

Happy to see his brother in such a good mood, Laksmana exclaimed, "Come, Rama! Surely such a glorious morning means that we will soon find Sita and rescue her!"

With that cheerful thought in mind, Rama and Laksmana laughed loudly and ran, stumbling, down the slope. Their voices resounded along the craggy pinnacle of the mountain as they tumbled and chuckled on their long descent, until, at last, they found themselves under the rich jungle canopy of the Valley of the Monkeys.

Seventeen

THE MARSHLANDS THAT STRETCHED along the flanks of the mountain teemed with life and spirited sounds as Rama and Laksmana made their way toward the Valley of the Monkeys. Slender trees rose from the rich murky waters, their trunks reaching high into the air, their ferny branches bowed under the weight of their abundant fruits. In the tranquil waters of countless pools swans, ducks, and herons serenely glided, sending up a happy cackle. The birds of this region knew nothing about fear, for they had never encountered human beings or hunters. They swam to the shore, coming very close to the brothers. Then they gazed at them with great curiosity and wonder, finding their unfurred and unfeathered human bodies rather strange.

Rama sang out a greeting to the birds, and they hissed and cackled merrily in reply.

"My friends," Laksmana inquired, "have you seen a

beautiful woman held captive by a fiend that dines on birds and butterflies? Have they come this way?" he asked.

The swans hissed and opened their wings wide in reply, but the brothers were unable to understand the language of birds. So they went on their way.

Just beyond the bog that meandered along the foot of the angry mountain, Rama and Laksmana suddenly came upon a fierce wasteland in which nothing lived and nothing grew. It seemed to them impossible that such desolation could exist in the midst of such profuseness. One moment they walked upon lush moss, and the next they stood in a wilderness of lifeless dunes. No plants or flowers could endure the burning sand and sweltering winds of this desolate place. The earth was mangled and scorched, as if a fiery meteor had plummeted into the marsh, burning and destroying everything in its path. What once had been a landscape filled with every kind of flower and beast was now sterile and poisoned, stretching out like a charred corpse in the relentless sun.

There was no dusk or dawn in this place. The cool and comforting night had fled and would not come again to this desolate land. Now there was just endless sun and heat. Now only the scorched earth.

Laksmana called out to Rama when he found in the burning sand the huge footprints of the demon Ravana.

"The monster was here! On this very spot!"

Across the deathly terrain were the burnt and blackened scars left by the fiery wheels of Ravana's chariot, marking the location where it had landed after careening from the sky. The broken and gnawed bones of birds were piled where Ravana had eaten and encamped. The ground still fumed and sputtered where the demon king of Lanka had walked. His tracks blemished the earth. Everywhere he had stepped the ground was parched, like a terrain that had been devastated by wildfire. Nothing grew and nothing survived the poison of his presence. Ravana had transformed this fertile strip of the marshlands into a wasteland. Everywhere was the long and lingering imprint of ashes and death.

Again Laksmana shouted to Rama, anxiously pointing to the only object of color that remained in the blotched and mutilated land. It was the bracelet Rama had given to Sita on their wedding day.

At the sight of the ornament, tears came to Rama's eyes.

But Laksmana was hopeful. "It is a good sign! She is still alive. She would never have parted with such a precious gift except to leave a trail for us to follow!"

The possibility that Sita might be held prisoner in the jungle filled the brothers with expectation. Though deeply depressed by the desolation left by Ravana's encampment and exhausted from their long day's march, Rama and Laksmana plunged with renewed energy into the legendary Valley of the Monkeys.

Everywhere were exotic blossoming trees . . . jambus

and panasas and nagas, filled with fruits and nuts. Laksmana jubilantly climbed into the great boughs, from which he hoped to catch a glimpse of the fertile valley.

"There is a lake!" he shouted down to Rama. "Just beyond this grove of trees. There is a truly splendid lake covered with lotuses and reeds."

"Perhaps Ravana is hiding there. Perhaps Sita is only a short distance away!" Rama exclaimed as he dashed into the tangle of vines and orchids without waiting for his brother to join him.

"Wait! Wait for me!" Laksmana shouted.

"There is not a moment to waste. Hurry, Laksmana. Hurry!"

As Rama and Laksmana rushed through the dense undergrowth, something crept silently among the ferns, its glowing eyes fixed upon the brothers as they raced headlong through the jungle's dense and endless wall of thorns and vines. Rama anxiously cried out in anticipation of finding Sita, and then, with caution, he stifled the sound with his hand, lest Ravana hear him. But the creature hiding in the thickets had already heard him, and it secretly leered at him from the murky depths of greenery. Its black nose twitched as it sniffed the air, catching the scent of Rama's blood that steamed from the scrapes opened by thorny creeping vines.

For a moment, Rama fell to his knees, gasping for breath. At once a blizzard of mosquitoes swarmed around him, feeding on his blood until he staggered back to his feet. Then, seeing the yellow glint of eyes peering at him from deep within the copse of ferns, he quickly made a gesture of caution to Laksmana.

But as suddenly as the eyes had appeared they vanished.

Fearing this meant that Ravana might be warned of their approach, the brothers continued carefully through the tangle of jungle.

Then the jungle itself disappeared. After Rama and Laksmana had lunged through a thicket of orchids and rosewood, they abruptly found themselves in the open. The vast and clouded sky stretched above. And before them, in a wide clearing, was a shimmering lake.

Laksmana slowly crouched, gesturing for Rama to follow his example, lest they be seen.

"Do you see something behind us, creeping in the bushes?" Laksmana whispered to his brother. "Just there . . . yellow eyes . . . over there . . . watching us."

"I have seen it," Rama murmured without looking in the direction of the intruder. "But it cannot be the demon, for it would have attacked without delay."

"What then can it be? And why does it hide itself from us?"

"I am not certain."

"Then we must be cautious," Laksmana whispered, slowly reaching for the sword that hung from his waist.

Just as Rama and Laksmana were about to creep back

into the cover of the dense network of leaves, a strange voice came from the jungle.

"Lord Rama, listen to what I am about to tell you," the husky voice said in a curious dialect.

Rama was startled by these words, for he was certain that only a demon could possess knowledge of his name.

"Come forward!" Rama commanded, catching sight once again of a pair of yellow eyes glowing in the darkness of the undergrowth. "If you value your life, come forward!" he shouted, drawing an arrow against the string of his powerful bow and aiming it into the bushes.

"You are in no danger from me," the voice said as glowing eyes came closer and the branches rustled under the weight of something heavy and huge advancing upon the brothers.

Then, to Rama's amazement, an enormous white ape lumbered from the thicket.

"You have enemies, but I am not one of them," the ape said. "If you will let me, I will be your friend."

Rama was about to kill the creature, but when he saw the wisdom and valor in the eyes of the enormous ape that hovered over him, he slowly lowered his bow. Even the ever-distrustful Laksmana stood in wonder at the nobility of the great white monkey.

"You are the royal brothers of Dasaratha," the creature said as he pointed one long black finger at Rama and Laksmana. "And I am called Hanuman."

"How do you know us?" Rama asked in confusion.

"A female creature very much like yourselves came here," the white monkey answered in a grave voice, crouching down among the orchids and gazing with sympathy at the brothers.

"Sita! It must have been Sita!" Laksmana cried.

"Where is that woman now?" urged Rama.

Hanuman nodded thoughtfully and gazed into the sky.

"She is gone . . . far away into the sky. Now she is gone, but many days ago the monkey folk saw her as she streaked across the sky in the clutches of a demon."

"Where did he take her?" Rama pleaded.

"That we do not know. We only know that she cried out to us, and we understood her call for help. The swans of Lake Pampa spread their powerful wings and flew to her rescue, but the monster encircled them in flames and they crashed to the ground. They were burnt and they were dying in misery, a misery that we have never known in the Valley of the Monkeys. But before the queen of the swans died, she turned to me, gasping that the strange female creature in the sky was one of us, for the swan queen had seen all the flowers of springtime in her wonderful eyes. So it was that the swan queen told me that this strange female creature cried out your names . . . Rama and Laksmana, the royal princes of a distant place called Dasaratha. But the swan queen could say no more, for she closed her eyes and died."

Rama looked at his brother. "We are too late . . ." he murmured dolefully. "We are always too late to save her. Now I begin to believe that we shall never see Sita again."

Hanuman placed his shaggy arms around Rama's shoulders and looked into his face with an expression so filled with compassion that Rama was moved to tears.

"Listen to what I tell you, Lord Rama," the white monkey said. "Not far from here there is a king named Sugriva. He is powerful and he is good, for he is the king of all the monkey people."

Laksmana was about to chuckle, but Rama restrained him with a disapproving glance.

"It is true," Hanuman said in his deep and mellow voice. "What I say is true. Sugriva is a great warrior. And he is also wise. I know he will be your friend and he will assist in searching for this female creature called Sita."

Laksmana was not convinced by these words of praise for the king of the monkeys.

"But what can a tribe of apes do to help us?" he whispered to Rama with a frown of misgivings.

Hanuman took no notice of Laksmana's belittling comment, but continued to urge Rama to win the alliance of Sugriva.

"Now is not the time for doubts," the white monkey counseled. "Forget all you know and think; instead think of all you do not know. Let us go together and seek powerful Sugriva. He will be your ally in ways beyond belief, for he has powers that will amaze you. He is able to change his form at will. The numberless monkey tribes of all the world will become your defenders and your army. Then, together, we will find Sita and rescue her!"

"But we cannot lay siege upon the demon unless we know where he is," Laksmana muttered, making no effort to conceal his considerable doubts about the merits of an army made up of monkeys. "Rama," Laksmana pleaded with his brother, "we must not linger here! We must go now before it is too late to find Sita."

"But where is it that you are going?" Hanuman asked as a keen golden light came into his ancient eyes. "In our jungle you are blind men, unable to find what you are searching for. But as long as the many-rayed sun shines, the monkey people will search every river, every crag, every inaccessible mountain and cave until we find the woman called Sita. King Sugriva will even venture into the bleak land of Ravana's own kingdom in faraway Lanka. For our king will understand that to save Sita is to save the earth! The demons that devour the forest will be destroyed! All this I promise to you."

Ignited by these hopeful words, Rama grasped the huge hairy hands of the white monkey.

"I believe you!" Rama exclaimed. "In your eyes I can see a distant reflection of Sita. In your voice I hear an echo of her voice!"

Then Rama turned to the reluctant Laksmana, saying,

"Brother, there is something here in the Valley of the Monkeys in which I believe. Put aside your doubts. Hanuman may be right. What can we know of the unknown if we are blinded by mistrust? We must learn to follow our hearts. And when I listen to my heart, it tells me that these creatures know what we do not know and see what we cannot see. Come! Put aside your vanity. Put aside your pride. And come with me to the king of the monkey people!"

"But brother . . ." Laksmana timidly murmured into Rama's ear, glancing hesitantly at Hanuman, "look at him. He is just an animal."

For a moment Rama smiled as a divine wisdom glowed in his marvelous eyes, and then he said, "Look into yourself, Laksmana, and there you will also find an animal."

Laksmana gave his brother an expression full of confusion and dismay.

"Come," Rama again urged in a whisper. "Take this journey with me. Perhaps such a hazardous and improbable adventure is all we can expect of a life fully lived."

In the Valley of the Monkeys it was always spring. The kutaja trees were perpetually in flower. The cold of winter could not find its way into the valley, and the heat of summer had lost its way long ago, never returning to the home of the monkey people. The jambu fruit, full of flavor, was a favorite among the creatures. Ripe mangoes, shaken by the breeze, fell to the ground. On the grassy slopes peacocks danced their wedding dances, gleaming in the moonlight. While in the sky circling flights of cranes, having fallen in love with the midnight clouds, formed a feathery necklace around the soft white shoulders of the moon.

Thunder echoed in the distance. A red deer lifted its head. The chief of the elephants, hearing the roar behind him, stopped in his tracks, and, always thirsting for a fight, turned back in fury, believing the thunder to be a young bull challenging his dominion.

Filled with humming bees, emerald-necked peacocks, and huge elephants in rut, the jungle and the night had a voice teeming with whispers and bellows. Dewdrops, like gems, fell into the folds of lush wide leaves, and the many-colored birds drank from them. In the silence, as the birds drank, the croaking of frogs could be heard in harmony with the rumbling thunder. The ferocious tigress peacefully slept in the grass as antelopes and forest goats meandered in her meadow, unafraid even when she opened one watchful eye and then sighed contentedly and fell back to sleep.

Now flocks of small yellow birds fluttered about the bright bronzed head of the monkey king, cooling his deeply furrowed brow. Awakened by the chatter of the birds, King Sugriva stretched and turned over in his ferny nest high in the nut trees. When he opened his eyes, throngs of monkeys, great and small, rose to their back legs, hooting and singing the night's song. Twisting and wriggling until their long, furry bodies turned first into elongated glimmers of light and then became a host of stars rising in jagged flashes across the darkening clouds. Now everywhere was the green song of the turning earth, humming the lullaby that summoned dreams and the ten thousand butterflies that fell asleep in the moonlit forest of the monkey king's eyes.

Into the blue light came the monkey king. He slowly descended from his nest, floating effortlessly among the tall reeds and dazzling flowers, followed dutifully by a procession of glimmering monkey-stars. Starlit hands gathered fruit in the blue light of the jungle. Starlit figures leaping in monkey dances, leaving a wide trail of laughter among the orchids and mango trees.

Then, abruptly, Hanuman and the princes of Dasaratha came into the clearing. The monkey king's dance ceased. The monkey folk fell silent. All eyes were on the strangers.

Without hesitation the monkey king gave a regal bow to Rama and Laksmana, gesturing for them to come near.

"I am Rama," the prince said with a gesture of great deference.

Sugriva the monkey king nodded attentively and waited for Rama to speak again.

"There was once a good king named Dasaratha," Rama said sorrowfully. "He ruled by love and love alone.

I, Rama, am the firstborn of Dasaratha, and this prince at my side is my brother, Laksmana. And my wife is called Sita. It is our search for my abducted wife that has brought us to your land."

"Then," said the king of the monkeys, "you are the ones for whom we have waited. Since the day the swans fell from the sky our tranquil forest has not been the same. Where once every flower and tree grew in abundance there is now a swath of waste and corruption burned into the foothills. A demon whose very breath was poisonous to our land has left the Valley of the Monkeys tearful and distressed. Where the demon landed, there is now only sterile sand. And when he flew away, he took a flower of such beauty and mystery that we sacrificed ourselves to save her from his grasp. And so, for all these many long seasons since we saw your wife, Sita, carried away, we have awaited your coming."

"I have come here in search of what I have lost," Rama murmured.

The monkey king nodded, fingering his long red whiskers and sinking deep in thought as the blue light in his eyes glowed.

"Say no more," the monkey king proclaimed, gesturing to the throng of monkeys that surrounded him. "We will join you in your search! Light the sacred fire. In its flames we will swear kinship to one another. We will awaken to the past that we have shared in the long memory of our land. And then we will form a mighty army of apes, and we will search all the world for Sita! And when we find her, we will destroy the monster that stole her, lest that demon murderer should survive and murder life itself!"

A shout of celebration arose from the great assembly. Then, without the slightest effort, the white ape called Hanuman took the royal brothers upon his massive shoulders and carried them toward the place where the sacred fire burned.

Eighteen

AN ARMY OF MONKEYS responded to the call of their king, Sugriva. With the help of the fleetest monkeys of his domain, the king summoned his tribe from every quarter of the world. Now a mighty throng, each led by its commander, spread out through the Valley of the Monkeys. Sugriva escorted Rama and Laksmana to the top of a towering summit, and then he ordered the commanders to parade their detachments, one by one, past the princes of Dasaratha.

As the gallant troops of monkeys of every description ceaselessly made their way before their king, even Laksmana was amazed by their numbers and their splendid skill and bravery. Rama's hopes rose as he watched the paraders . . . hundreds at a time, unit after unit of disciplined warriors, disappearing from his view and raising an enormous cloud of dust with their marching feet.

Rama smiled at his brother. "It is time to start our siege!" he jubilantly exclaimed.

As dusk began to turn the jungle into a labyrinth of dark wonders—flitting shadows and shimmering specks of light—all the monkey commanders met with King Sugriva, Rama, and Laksmana, conducting a solemn council of war.

"My soldiers will be your scouts," King Sugriva told Rama and his brother. "While we wait here, my commanders will go in search of the demon. For the monkey captains know this land well."

So Sugriva sent armies to the east and to the west. He also sent many strong warriors to the far north. But to the south he sent the noble Hanuman and his second-in-command, a handsome ape called Angada. For Sugriva knew that the lands south of the Valley of the Monkeys, where even the dead feared to go, was the most likely place to find Ravana and his captive Sita.

Before the night descended, the wise monkey king gave Hanuman and Angada an insight into the strange worlds they would discover beyond the Valley of the Monkeys.

"As the old stories tell us, when you leave our valley, you will first rise into the clouded mountains in the south. And then you will travel onward to the river of blood where the crocodiles, giant fruit bats, and leopards have their home. Beyond the dense jungle that lies across the river you will find something called the sea, an expanse of water so great that crossing it defies even the most cunning and crafty of our tribe. But just off our shore, rising from the salty water, you will find a tortuous rock in the shape of a monkey's skull. It is there that the wicked Ravana dines on monkey brains and butterfly wings. Though this terrible little island is far from Ravana's kingdom in Lanka, it is there in dark caves that he often hides from the purity of our moon, lest she blind him with the radiance of her immaculate light!"

These words of instruction Sugriva gave to Hanuman in particular, for he was supremely confident that this valiant leader, the foremost of monkeys, would be the commander to find Sita.

"Think well," the king murmured to Hanuman, "how you will devise a scheme to bring Sita back to us. You must consider how the wondrous Sita will respond when she sees Hanuman coming to her defense. How will she know that you come at the behest of Rama? For she could mistake your purpose despite her knowledge of all creatures that exist in our jungle."

"That is true," agreed Laksmana with alarm. "Sita may believe some demon has taken Hanuman's form in order to delude her! She may refuse to come away with him! What then will happen, Rama?"

Rama nodded thoughtfully, and then he took from his wrist Sita's bracelet that he had found on the ground, placing it in Hanuman's massive hand.

"By this bracelet," Rama said, "Sita will know you to be my true messenger."

Hanuman grasped the bracelet in his fist and held it

high in the darkening sky as he proudly turned to face his army of monkeys. His gesture drew a rousing and optimistic cheer from the hardy troops.

Now, under the orders of their sovereign, all the monkey leaders departed in great haste to join their brigades. Then they ventured fearlessly in the directions assigned to them.

Suddenly there was the thunderous sound of marching feet. And, full of valor, their numberless legions moved forward with a great uproar, shouting, howling, and chattering as they went.

The king of the monkeys serenely dozed in his ferny nest in the treetops, secure in the knowledge that he had saved his royal guests from danger by forbidding them to accompany his troops. But Rama remained wakeful as he nervously awaited news of victory or defeat from the monkey commanders.

Laksmana tried to comfort his brother.

"You yourself said what fine warriors they are!" he exclaimed with a great show of confidence. "And you saw them march away by the thousands! How can you doubt that they will find Sita and bring her back to us?"

But Rama knew that his brother was exaggerating his trust in the military skill of the monkey army in the hope of bringing comfort to him. For when Rama looked into

Laksmana's face, he could detect a depth of doubt and worry no less than his own.

The days and nights passed, and the brothers became increasingly anxious.

There was no word.

There were no messengers.

"Your Majesty," Laksmana called up to the monkey king, "while you sleep we wait! Where are the messengers your commanders promised to send us?"

"You are a curious breed . . . you naked creatures without fur or feathers," Sugriva grunted as he opened one eye and glanced down from his nest. "You think that time is supposed to perform tricks for you. You think that everything in the world will sit up and beg or roll over and play dead for you. But time is time, my impatient young friend, and there is nothing in the world that you can do to change its pace. Not even your unmanageable eagerness will influence time. So go to sleep and leave me in peace."

With this retort, the monkey king rolled over and closed his eyes.

Laksmana was visibly irritated by the king's remarks, but Rama calmed him.

"Sugriva is right," Rama murmured. "We are tired and cranky and overwrought. We should try to sleep. Perhaps tomorrow word of Sita will finally come."

Already the sky was brightening with dawn when the

brothers lay down and tried to sleep. Then suddenly, just as they were closing their eyes, the voice of a messenger rang out in the jungle.

Rama and Laksmana jumped to their feet and anxiously awaited the exhausted monkey who dashed toward them through the undergrowth.

"Have you found Sita?" Laksmana shouted eagerly.

"Let the poor fellow catch his breath," the monkey king admonished as he slowly descended from his nest.

When the exhausted monkey was able to speak, he did so with a look of mortification in his eyes.

"The commander of the north sends me," he gasped. "We have traveled to the very end of the northern world, but there was no trace of Sita. We searched every cave, every summit, every valley, and yet we found not a single creature that had seen the beautiful Sita."

Rama sighed with great despair as he turned away sadly.

"That is nonsense!" Laksmana exclaimed with irritation. "Surely your quest to the north revealed something!"

"Nothing . . ." the messenger whispered. "We did our best, but we found nothing."

"No one can ask more of you," the wise king of the monkeys murmured as he touched the melancholy messenger upon his shoulder. "Now go and feed yourself and sleep. Perhaps tomorrow there will be better news from the west."

But when dawn brightened the sky the next morning, and when another messenger hastened to give Sugriva his report, he too conceded that the commander sent to the farthest reaches of the western region had found no trace of Sita.

And again, at the dawning of the next day, the messenger from the east had the same bad news. Sita was nowhere to be found.

"That leaves only Angada and Hanuman, who marched south more days ago than I can remember. For all we know, they may be lost forever," Laksmana muttered when the messenger from the east had imparted his sad news.

"I think not," mused the king of the monkeys. "I think not."

Sugriva was right. When the moon had made herself into a large, round, and shining lantern in the sky, there came a stirring in the jungle. The birds were awakened from their sleep. The tigers growled and the elephants grunted. And finally, Hanuman, the white monkey, lumbered into the presence of his king.

But Sita was not in his company.

"Tell us," Sugriva gently urged, when Hanuman had eaten and had glumly taken a seat with Rama and Laksmana in the light of the sacred fire, "what news do you bring us?"

"The news is not good, my lords," Hanuman said in a sullen voice. "We searched the rocks and the hiding places of owls and rabbits. We asked every bird and every beast if Sita had come its way, but everywhere we were told that such a beautiful creature was unknown to the tribes of the south."

"Ah," cried Rama with a weariness so great that tears came into the eyes of even stalwart Laksmana.

"After many days and nights," Hanuman continued, "we came to the great water of which you told us. A lake gone mad, boundless and fantastic. So vast it was unbelievable. Like an eternal and featureless paradise where time and water entwined. That is what we found. And where we thought to find a demon, we found only our own faces reflected in the water. And where we thought to find the kingdom of evil Ravana, we found only the world's end, beyond which we could not venture. And so, my lords, I stood on the shore, gazing in confusion at the wide water, staring toward the far horizon in an effort to understand the endlessness of what stretched before me. Seeing what I could not comprehend. Yet knowing it stood before me. A sea so vast that it was no longer clear to me what it was or what it meant. I tried, but, my lords, I could not understand it. And so I have returned to you in defeat and despair."

"In all this while, you found nothing?" Laksmana exclaimed in exasperation. *"Nothing?"*

Hanuman bowed his head. Then he said, "We found only the fearsome rock in the water called Monkey Skull. And we found a great bird called Sampathi, whose wings were seared and whose spirit was broken. He had come to defend all the tribes of birds from a monster, but he failed. The demon engulfed him in fire and singed his wings so he could no longer fly. Everywhere were the bloody feathers of ten thousand birds. And, my lords, everywhere were the piled bones of our monkey people. Devoured. Destroyed and consumed by Ravana!"

For a long time, Hanuman and the royal brothers sat in silence, vacantly staring into the flames of the sacred fire.

Then the king of the monkeys arose and said, "A sad story . . . it is indeed a very sad story. But Hanuman, my friend, our quest for Sita is not yet over. We must seek the help of Sampathi, for I know that magical bird very well. Four thousand years ago, when he and I were young, he used to carry me into the air so I could see all there was to see of the heavens and the earth. He is gallant and wise, and I am certain that he will assist us. His powerful wings were so huge and wide that he could fly high above the Valley of the Monkeys and far beyond the great water. For even that endless sea must end, though we cannot imagine it. And where that magnitude of water ceases is where we shall find Sita, because she has been carried by the demon to a place beyond our imaginations. That much I know for certain. Our troops, with all their efforts, have not found her in the east, west, north, nor even in the fantastic lands of the south. So she is somewhere beyond the earth we know. Only

Sampathi can see what we cannot see, for he guards the gate that stands between what is here and what is there. If any creature has seen Sita or the demon Ravana, it will be Sampathi."

Hanuman was surprised by his king's admiration for the bird he had seen. Sampathi had been so singed and dispirited.

"But he is such a pitiable vulture," Hanuman murmured. "I doubt that he can ever again rise into the air or soar the unthinkable distance that lies between what is here and what is there."

The king of the monkeys smiled as he slowly bit into a ripe mango, sitting back on his haunches and gazing first at Hanuman and then at Rama and Laksmana. When he had savored the sweetness of the fruit of the earth, his smile of pleasure widened and a tiny spark suddenly ignited in midair. Then there appeared a trace of blue light, filling Sugriva's ancient eyes. This light grew into a blazing figure of radiant illumination that streamed outward in every direction, filling the night, joining hands with the moonlight and dancing away into the jungle, where it awakened every creature. Soon the night resounded with bellows, roars, hoots, and howls.

"Hear me, my friends of feather and fur!" exclaimed the king of the monkeys, who gleamed under a festoon of glimmering lights. "Fly away! Go in every direction! Fly away and bring my words to all the monkey people!"

As the monkey king spoke, a single bird flew toward

him and perched on his bright red head. Then another and another bird appeared, until there was such a rustling and fluttering of wings coming from the outer darkness of the world that it sounded like the invasion of a billion locusts.

Birds filled the air. Millions upon millions of many-colored birds, chirping and flapping. So many birds that they darkened even the brilliant figure of blue light that gallantly embraced the moonlight in a fantastic dance in the sky.

"Fly! Now fly away, my friends," Sugriva commanded as the birds soared into the sky, flitting in every direction. "And tell my mighty monkey warriors that we shall meet at the place where the great water begins!"

In a moment, the birds were gone. Their fluttering wings vanished, leaving the vast night sky motionless and empty. Sugriva's splendid blue light madly whirled and whirled into the clearing, flashing upward momentarily before it streaked down upon the monkey king and disappeared into his body.

Now the night was silent. Now the moon slipped behind a cloud. Leaving only darkness. Now a single firefly darted into the misty sky. Flitting in the empty air. Beaming. Brightly gleaming. While from the distance came the ever-trilling song of a night bird. Singing.

Nineteen

*E*VERYWHERE WAS THE SEA. Rama stood at the water's edge, amazed by its enormity. He cried out to the vast expanse of water that swelled and swirled before him, but there was no answer.

The sea was the sea. It stretched out in the bright sun and sighed its everlasting sigh, but it took no notice of Lord Rama.

Rama muttered in disappointment and dismay, for he could not imagine how he would lead his vast army of monkeys across such an expansive and treacherous waterway. The more he gazed into the glistening horizon, the more dejected he became. He had come so far and he had searched so long that he could not believe his search for Sita would end in defeat. But it could not be otherwise, for the ocean would not yield to him.

As he stared out into the distance, envisioning Sita held captive in a distant and barbarous land, he grew melancholy. Forlorn and miserable, Rama stood at the edge of the swirling surf. He raised his arms, pleading for the sea to make way for his troops.

The ocean lazily turned in its vast bed of sand, and then it whispered, "Behold, the sea. Behold! Cradle of life. Ancient as the stars. Hear me. Hear me, Lord Rama. I beckon to all, but I answer to none. The streams and creeks rush through high mountain passes and long valleys in answer to my call. The rivers and brooks, tumbling through canyons and ravines, hurry to me, dreaming of my eternal embrace. The fragile rain that rises from my bosom in the heat of summer, held captive in black clouds, longs for the lightning to set it free, so it can come home to me. Hear me. Hear me. You go no farther. This is the edge of the world. Leave me, Rama. Do not awaken me from my ceaseless slumber."

Enraged by the ocean's unwillingness to surrender to him, Rama lifted his bow, threatening to shoot his fiery arrows into the depths so all the mighty waters of the world would vaporize and vanish, and all of the mysterious creatures of the deep would perish.

"I fear nothing from your threats!" roared the sea. "I am eternal and know nothing of death! Why do you waste your feeble hostility upon eternity?"

"I will risk even the wrath of eternity to recover my wife, Sita!" sobbed Rama, falling to his knees.

At the very mention of Sita's name the ocean swelled. Rain pelted the churning tide. A rainbow arched in the sunlit sky. And the exuberant dance of the waves stirred the very depths, so that strands of lush seaweed and iridescent jellyfish and emerald turtles floated to the gleaming surface amidst bubbles and foam pregnant with fragile life not yet lived.

"*Sita . . .*" sang the sea. "She is my body. She is my shore."

Lightning ripped across the horizon. A sudden wind blew the waves into cascades of froth.

"Where is Sita now?" the water sang out as the waves danced in the turbulent surge. "She dwelled in the earth as I dwell in the sea. But now Sita is gone. Pity the world, Prince Rama. Pity the world. For Sita is gone. And if she does not soon return, the earth will endure a season without blossoms or blooms. The tender roots of spring will die in the mouth of winter."

Rama sighed and tears came into his eyes.

"Then it is true," he muttered in dread. "Even the sea admits what I will not admit. Sita is forever lost. Somewhere in the wild world she is lost and cannot be found. And with her has gone all the happiness of my life!"

"Ah . . ." hissed the surf in misery and anguish as it slowly withdrew into itself, leaving only a forsaken strand of lifeless sand.

"Tell me, lord of the sea," Rama begged. "You saw Sita abducted! But did you see her die?"

"I saw only the demon fleeing with her in his clutches," sighed the water.

"Then she may still be alive!" exclaimed Rama. "For if

Sita were safely carried beyond your endless waters, then she may yet survive as a prisoner in some barbaric land!"

"Taken away she was," groaned the sea. "But where she is, I do not know. So pity the world. For if Lord Rama does not know where Sita is held captive, then how can all the armies of the world rescue her?"

When the ocean had said these hopeless words, there came a whimper from the sand dunes that surrounded the shore. Then the wretched bird called Sampathi crawled to the water's edge, where he lay upon his belly and gazed with great wonder at Lord Rama.

"Once . . ." Sampathi groaned as he spread the pathetic stubs of his once-wide wings, "long ago . . . before the demon's fiery breath destroyed my lovely plumes, my wings were as wild as the winter moon and as strong as summer's sun. On my broad wings I could soar high and wide. Over the great water I could fly, into the horizon and beyond all that is known."

"Yes," murmured Rama as he looked at the wretched creature. "I know this sad story and I know your name, for Hanuman, the commander of the monkey army, spoke of you when he returned from his quest for Sita."

Sampathi struggled to his crippled feet and limped toward Rama.

"Were I but whole again, Lord Rama, I would fly into the fearsome night beyond the night . . . into the dark world where Sita vanished!"

With these heroic words, the great bird became silent, weeping in misery as it gazed at its seared and blackened plumage.

Rama was so touched by Sampathi's devotion to Sita that he gently touched the enormous bird upon its featherless head.

Sampathi cried out in pain.

Suddenly a blinding shower of sparks flew upward, igniting the air and sending up billows of dark smoke.

Again the great bird shouted in torment.

Rama quickly withdrew his hand from Sampathi's head, fearing that his very touch had killed the poor creature. But when the smoke vanished, Rama was amazed to see a marvelous sight. There before him stood an immense bird of glorious-colored plumage, its handsome head held high, its yellow eyes filled with wisdom.

"Rama," Sampathi cried with delight, "I live again!"

For indeed, the great bird had been miraculously reborn by the compassion of Lord Rama's simple gesture.

"Now," exclaimed Sampathi as he flapped his wide wings, making a powerful wind as he leaped into the air, "just as I vowed, I go in search of Sita!"

The ocean leaped into foaming waves as Sampathi glided upward and gradually grew smaller and smaller as he flew into the horizon. Then he was gone.

Now Rama was alone with the inexhaustible sea.

In the silence, the great water whispered to the prince.

"Hear me, Lord Rama. Since it is Sita for whom you search, then I too will help you in your quest. The unyielding sea yields to the hero who revives the spring. So go in haste and assemble your great army. Only then will you be able to walk upon the lofty waves without drowning in my swift currents. Whatever earth and timbers you bring to my invincible shores, those things I will hold firmly upon my tides so they will neither sink nor be engulfed by the depths. And when you have made a sturdy bridge for your monkey warriors, I will calm the waves, and they will arch their powerful backs to hold your bridge aloft. This I promise, Prince Rama!"

The mighty ocean thundered as it rose from its deep bed and opened its watery arms to Rama.

Hearing the news that the sea was their ally in the search for Sita, a massive assembly of monkeys gathered on the shore. Their chatter and howls filled the air as their leaders instructed them to search the forests and mountains for a great quantity of massive boulders and the sturdy trunks of dead trees with which the bridge across the water could be built.

Soon the miraculous bridge began to take shape, stretching slowly out into the impassable ocean. And just when the energy of the monkey warriors began to wane, the great bird Sampathi appeared in the sky, eagerly sweeping down to the beach where Rama stood with his brother, Laksmana.

"I have found Sita!"

A shout of joy rose into the wind. Hanuman climbed to the top of the tallest tree at the forest's edge, and from there he announced to the multitude of warriors that Sita was imprisoned in a small garden guarded by the henchmen of the demon Ravana.

At the very mention of the name of the monster who had feasted on the bodies of their simian kinsmen, the monkeys hooted in rage, prancing and grunting as they beat their chests and showed their long sharp teeth.

Without delay they sent up a call to all the members of their tribe, vowing that the great causeway across the water would be finished by the sixth day of their labors. Then every monkey returned to work with an energy and strength never before known in the Valley of the Monkeys.

So great was their labor that every creature and every bird of the forest came to witness the monkeys' incredible feat of construction. Soon these spectators became so enthralled by the pandemonium that they gleefully joined in the work.

Bears put their broad shoulders to immense boulders and laboriously pushed them to the end of the almost-finished causeway. Even the squirrels gathered large and small pebbles and scurried with them to the water's edge. Fish owls and laughing thrushes and saffron orioles busily gathered anything they could carry in their beaks and claws, and then they swooped down upon the causeway, where they released a downpour of thatch, sticks, and reeds upon the rock foundation.

Finally, the bridge was completed. The animals were jubilant, splashing in the shallow water, dancing upon the shore, flitting in the air, hooting, chirping, and bellowing as they gazed at their magnificent achievement.

A vast causeway upon the waves. It was so long that it vanished into the haze that gathered upon the far horizon. A glorious bridge spanning the great water. A gleaming white line on the murky sea, like the parting of a woman's dark hair.

In a splendid cloak of yellow flowers and crimson grasses, Sugriva, king of the monkeys, moved majestically into the throng. A hush fell upon the endless rows of creatures as Sugriva and his ministers silently made their way to the shore. Then, as Sugriva placed one foot upon the causeway and raised his arms in triumph, a great cheer arose from the crowd.

"Now is the time, brothers and sisters, for us to confront the monster that slays and devours us! Hunted no more! Victims no more! Now is the time for Rama and Laksmana to lead our armies to the forbidden land of Lanka, where Sita is held captive in an eternal winter. So beware, wicked Ravana, for we come to claim your terrible heart!"

A deafening cheer resounded over the water as the monkeys marched forward, beating upon log drums and piping on bamboo flutes. In the lead was Hanuman, carrying Rama on his shoulders, followed by Angada, who bore Laksmana on his back. Then came the numberless legions of warriors, howling and hooting as they pressed steadily along the wide and sturdy causeway. So terrific was the tumult of the tramping feet of the army of monkeys that it drowned out the roar of the mighty sea.

Now the multitude grew silent as the skies darkened. The waves groaned in pain as they washed upon the austere and jagged stones that flanked the barren shore of Lanka. In the bitter darkness of a perpetual winter the troops slowly moved across the ribbon of stone and timber that spanned the sea, gazing in dread at the desolate land they found on the dark side of the world.

The tide reeked of stagnation and death. The water was awash with rotting fish floating in a thick scum of tar and oil. Just beyond the strand decayed and leafless trees stood bent and miserable in a ravaged thicket in which there were no birds or flowers.

Darkness everywhere.
A moonless sky filled with wailing and wind.
Shadows.
Fearsome shadows.

And glistening eyes peering out of the perpetual night.

A dead land. Torn and ravished by greedy hands.

A world of clammy mists and caustic rain that burned the eyes.

The gloomy sky choking on ashes and soot. And everywhere a bruised and broken land defiled by monsters.

Barren and bereft of creatures.

Smoldering fires and smoke billowing from the stained rocks of a ruined temple where demons in the bloody skins of animals worshiped every evil and every wickedness.

Animal bones piled high around dreadful altars.

Sacrificial corpses limply hanging from the sharp antlers of a huge, blackened skull, its voracious mouth gaping, its hollow eyes filled with death.

This terrible and desolate realm was the kingdom of Ravana, the demon king of Lanka.

At the first sound of the advancing army of monkeys the eyes vanished like falling stars streaking through the night. The figures of the terrible sacrificial priests shimmered in the putrid air. Then they billowed upward and fled like dark clouds blown across a forsaken sky.

So devastated and austere was the land of Lanka that the massive surge of monkey warriors faltered, murmuring in astonishment at the plundered landscape they saw spread before them. Then they suddenly came to a halt.

In the stillness, Rama, who was perched on Hanuman's shoulder, urged him to move closer to the shore.

The gigantic ape hesitated and then, with great caution, he carried Rama to the very edge of the causeway, closely followed by the monkey commander Angada, who bore Laksmana on his back.

Rama and Laksmana vigilantly climbed down to the bridge and stood in a remorseful silence as they looked into the ravaged land that stretched out like a corpse before them.

Rama closed his eyes and, from his heart, he summoned all his courage.

"I will not risk your lives, my friends," Lord Rama announced. "It is I alone who wished to go in search of Sita. And though my faithful brother has vowed to accompany me, and though the monkey people and all the creatures of the forest have sworn to be our allies, it is I alone who must first set foot into this terrible kingdom of death and decay. For this battle is my battle. And if there is one of us who is to be the first to die, then that person must be Rama!"

With these words, Prince Rama slowly stepped from the protection of the bridge onto the seething soil of Lanka.

At once, fierce flames shot from the ground, flashing in the air like blazing daggers that bore down upon Rama. As the blaze surrounded the prince, a fearful gasp arose like a troubled wind from the monkey ranks.

But Lord Rama quickly drew his magic bow and sent an arrow into the menacing fire, sending the flames fleeing in wretched smoke and dying embers.

Rama strode heroically forward, to the cheers of the troops.

"Beware, Ravana!" the prince shouted as he planted his sword deep into the defiled soil of Lanka that had forever lost the delight of springtime. "Your evil magic cannot stop us. We come to wound your wicked heart and to bring an end to your endless winter!"

Carried away by the gallantry of the huge assembly of warriors, Laksmana rushed to his brother's side.

"Let me bring word to Ravana that he must surrender or perish!" Laksmana implored. "Let me be your messenger!"

But Rama could not bear the thought of his defenseless brother facing the vile sorceries of the king of Lanka.

"We are the princes of Dasaratha," Rama murmured, embracing his brother. "Our glory has already been won for this day. For it was in the name of Dasaratha that I planted my sword in the soil of Lanka. Now Dasaratha must yield to its allies. And so I give homage to the king of the monkeys by appointing his great commander Angada to take our message to Ravana."

Laksmana was disheartened by his brother's decision. But he smiled when Angada exclaimed, "I will do what I have been honored to do, but let me go to Ravana with Laksmana at my side!"

The vast assembly cheered with approval.

Then King Sugriva stepped forward to embrace Rama. "Let it be as Rama commands," the king proclaimed. "The mortal Laksmana of Dasaratha will go with Angada of the monkey people. But the great bird Sampathi will accompany them, as will the bear called Jambavan, whose people pushed great boulders into the sea, and the squirrel named Gouh, whose tribe carried pebbles and stones to the bridge, and the small bird called Bulbul, whose flocks brought twigs and thatch to surface the great causeway. Let all be represented when Ravana is given Rama's ultimatum!"

With shouts of approval, the chosen messengers rushed forward to take their places beside Laksmana and Angada. Then, with the beating of log drums and the piping of bamboo flutes, the appointed couriers began their precarious journey to the dreadful palace of Lord Ravana.

In the terrible shower of acid rain and the smothering darkness, Rama and the great white monkey Hanuman waited anxiously for their return. All around them on the barren shore the warrior monkeys spread out, noisily encamping on the tainted strand, where they dined on the nuts and berries they had brought with them into this fruitless land.

After many days of worry for the survival of the messengers, the encampment was startled by the sound of Sampathi's flapping wings.

"I bring you news!" the great bird exclaimed as it swooped down amongst the excited warriors and hurried to the place where he was eagerly awaited by Rama, Hanuman, and King Sugriva.

"What news is this?" urged Hanuman.

"All are safe despite Ravana's wrath!" Sampathi announced.

"But where is my brother, Laksmana?" Rama beseeched.

"And where is Angada?" Sugriva implored.

"Even now they come over the crest just behind me!" exclaimed Sampathi.

As he spoke, the exhausted bird Bulbul dashed headlong through the air, flitting about Rama's head. Next the squirrel rushed into the crowd, scampering between Sugriva's feet. And from the distance could be heard the bellows of the bear and the shouts of Laksmana and Angada.

When Laksmana had caught his breath, he was chosen to give the report of the adventures of the messengers.

"As Rama commanded," he told the apprehensive assembly, "we made our way to Ravana, a demon more terrible than any monster in the world! And then, showing no hint of fear or intimidation, mighty Angada stepped forward and told Ravana that Rama sends warning that his doom is at hand."

The great ape called Angada bowed his head in

183

humility as the monkey warriors sent up a shout in his honor.

Then Laksmana continued. "It was now my turn to face the demon. And so I too stepped forward and told him that despite our warning it was not too late for him to restore Sita and to beg Rama's forgiveness."

Now Jambavan the huge bear lumbered to Rama's side, and with a leer on his thin, black lips, he said, "Ravana ordered all of us to be killed at once!"

"Ah," murmured Rama.

"But it was more easily said than done." Laksmana laughed.

"When the demons came to seize us," Sampathi exclaimed, "Angada rose to his full height, towering above even the monster Ravana. And with a roar Angada grabbed hold of our executioners and tucked them under his powerful arms. Then he leaped so high into the sky that he toppled the tower of Ravana's gloomy palace. And from the heights he flung the demons down upon the broken stones of the ruined tower!"

"So stunned were the demons that we were able to flee from them without injury!" Laksmana proclaimed.

"And Sita? What of my beloved wife, Sita?" Rama asked with great urgency.

"She is safe, my lord," Sampathi assured him.

"She is held prisoner in a garden," Laksmana explained in a voice full of indignation. "For now she is safe."

Rama and King Sugriva listened intently to all that was reported to them, and then they joined in a council of war, speaking to each other in grim whispers, while the monkey and bear warriors anxiously awaited their leaders' decision.

Now King Sugriva turned to the massive army that stretched in every direction as far as he could see.

"Arm yourselves! Gather your strength! And light your torches!" commanded the king of the monkeys. "For now, without delay, we go to confront Ravana!"

The exhilarated voices of the monkeys and bears and birds resounded in the dismal sky, filled with gales of burning rain that fell upon the exhausted land like blood.

Soon the eternal twilight of Lanka was lighted by the sputtering flames of countless torches that moved across the dark landscape like stars in the heavens.

"To Ravana's palace!" shouted Rama as the huge white ape, Hanuman, lifted him to his shoulder.

"To the gates of the tyrant!" exclaimed Laksmana from the brawny back of the monkey commander Angada.

The invaders sent up an exalted noise as they marched into the blackness of the wasteland that surrounded Ravana's palace.

Now it was neither night nor day. Fearful shadows slowly enveloped the scorched earth. Rust and slime oozed over the lifeless soil, seething among the jagged splinters of mountains shattered by yellow-eyed monsters who belched soot and cinders as they tore through the agonized ground, leaving only stagnant pools of mud and the stumps of dead trees. Carcasses and cadavers smoldered among the heaps of burning refuse, billowing sulfurous vapor, invading the lifeless world with the overwhelming stench of death and decay. The animal tracks had vanished. There were no birds in the sky. And the wind had died in the poisonous clouds that hovered over the suffocated earth.

The sky was full of turbulent flashes of light and flames. Humble houses once occupied by contented farmers now lay in smoldering heaps. The peasants fled in an interminable stream of exhausted refugees, leaving the weak and the sick behind to face the night alone. Now nothing remained of the happy people who had been the natives of Lanka before the demon Ravana had come from the sky to feast on their bodies and to destroy their lands.

People with faces full of numbed horror and inexpressible pain stumbled blindly among the ruins, muttering to themselves, dragging the bodies of their lifeless children. Towering walls swayed, tottered, and fell upon them, and they died without a sound. Buried in the dust and rubble. Arms . . . legs protruding from the piles of stones.

Silent.

Those who were not crushed slouched on without looking back. Trudging into the smoke and fog, defenseless against the black, growling demons who darted out of the darkness and carried them away. Their numbers diminishing each day of the endless flight from Lord Ravana. Still they went on, stopping only to drink from the poisoned streams, where animals and people lay dead, their featureless faces submerged in the murky water.

Silent. Silent.

No sobs. No weeping.

Nothing but death and silence.

And in the midst of such agony, the army of monkeys marched onward to the palace of Ravana.

Rama wept when he witnessed the plight of the brutalized people fleeing their doomed country. His tears fell upon the sterile ground, and where they fell the stones flinched like wounded beasts under the whip of a cruel master.

The world became darker and darker as the army advanced into the desolation of Lanka. Evil omens were everywhere. Hot winds blew across the stern faces of the warriors. The earth trembled and the mountains quaked. The lifeless trunks of tall trees crashed to the ground. Sinister clouds resembling birds of prey swooped through the air with terrifying screams, letting loose a deluge of rain mixed with blood. The sky, red and pulsating like a beating heart, loomed above, filled with unspeakable horrors . . . shadows with serpent heads and eagle wings and wide jaws glistening with sharp teeth.

The piles of corpses were everywhere, slowly dissolving in the pitiless rain. The earth changed to mud and gore. And into the spirits of the courageous monkey warriors there slowly crept a haunting feeling of fear and loathing.

"We go no farther!" exclaimed Rama from his perch high on Hanuman's shoulders.

The monkeys, filled with fatigue and dreadful premonitions, anxiously responded to Rama's commands. They halted before the gates of Lanka.

Deadly silence.

Nothing stirred.

No one in sight.

Only the lonely sigh of the hot wind and the growling of the angry clouds could be heard in the continual pelting of the bloody rain.

Rama peered cautiously into the black mist that rose like a wall against the battlements of the palace of Lanka.

King Sugriva gave a silent signal to Hanuman and Angada, who advanced a few wary steps and then lifted Rama and Laksmana from their backs.

Nothing.

Only whistling wind and the faint cry of dying creatures somewhere in the distance.

Perhaps, thought Rama, *the enemy is invisible.*

Now Rama, bow in hand, crept forward with his brother, Laksmana, close behind him.

When they reached the putrid moat that oozed along the outer walls of the palace, Rama carefully peered up at the impregnable northern gate, which was as high as the peak of a mountain.

Meanwhile the great bear Jambavan stealthily took up his position at the eastern gate at the head of a host of burly bear warriors.

Angada with his vast monkey forces occupied the southern gate. While Hanuman was stationed at the western gate with thousands of soldiers grouped closely around him.

Now, in an anxious silence, the throngs of troops awaited the signal from King Sugriva to charge the gates and begin the battle. Lashing their tails feverishly, the monkeys licked their teeth and claws, which they would use as fierce weapons against the demons. Trembling expectantly in every limb, their faces were set in grim expressions, fearful but eager to fight.

At last the signal was given. In the light of ten thousand torches King Sugriva raised his arms.

The earth and the air filled with creatures rushing toward the gates of Lanka. By the hundreds and the hundreds of thousands, bears and birds and monkeys and every other creature laid siege upon the walls of the palace of the demon Ravana. The noise of the attack was so great that the ramparts, arches, and sturdy walls of the palace began to tremble.

"Victory to King Sugriva!" yelled the monkeys as they set fire to the massive gates.

Fearing the safety of Sita during the attack, Sampathi leaped into the air and swept high over the palace walls, seeking the garden where Rama's wife was held captive.

No sooner had Sampathi vanished than flames of the palace gates shot upward in a burst, blazing with such fury that the dark landscape was flooded with flickering light. When the protective doors were crumbling in smoldering embers, the bears lifted huge tree trunks upon their shoulders and rushed at the flaming entrances, pummeling them again and again with the logs. Finally all the gates gave way, and there came a triumphant cry of the warriors as the blazing barriers came crashing down.

The fires quickly died into glowing ashes. Darkness poured down upon the world as Rama peered through the gutted gateways into the black interior of Ravana's vile realm.

Still blinded by the ferocity of the flames, Rama could not see anything but motionless shadows hovering just within the walls of Lanka. He slowly raised his hand, and the warriors who flocked close behind him fell utterly silent.

In the silence Rama could hear the muffled breathing of a thousand monsters hidden in the darkness just beyond the collapsed gates of the palace.

For a long moment, the warriors stood in anxious

silence, gazing with dread into the lightless eyes of the demons that stirred in the shadows just beyond them. Then King Sugriva gave a bellowing battle cry, and suddenly the invaders pushed forward; while from every side a deafening clamor arose from the army of monkeys. They screeched and shrieked as they threw their torches into the shadows, causing a brilliant fire to explode in the darkness.

Now, in the torchlight, Rama could see his terrible enemies for the first time. Gigantic beings with flapping elephant ears and long jagged tusks and gaping mouths overflowing with crimson saliva. Glowing eyes filled with oblivion. Six arms writhing like snakes. The feet of jackals and the bodies of tigers. Their faces still bloodied from gorging themselves on the bodies of living creatures.

Then, without warning, a fierce counterattack began. The demons lurched forward with wails and growls so violent and terrible that the monkeys momentarily recoiled in fear. But King Sugriva's war cries urged them forward into the tide of stampeding demons.

The monkey troops fought with astonishing ferocity, hurling themselves at their enemies with complete abandon. Assaulting their gruesome foes with logs and stones and bamboo spears, the monkeys pressed steadily into the midst of the swarm of monsters, bombarding them with such force that the demons stumbled and fell to the ground, bleeding streams of putrid, green blood and calling to their fellow demons for help.

That help was quick to come. Suddenly the monkeys were bombarded by lances, darts, and poisoned arrows. Careening war chariots pulled by huge spiders crashed into the monkey troops, tossing their bodies in every direction.

The two armies mercilessly pounded at each other, creating a bloody tangle of writhing bodies. In the ensuing fracas many fearsome hand-to-hand duels arose between the monsters and the most heroic of the forest creatures.

Angada lifted a stout tree trunk and whirled it around again and again, sending demons flying into the air. Hanuman leaped upward and then came crashing down on his enemies. King Sugriva drove his sword into the heartless breasts of the monsters. While Laksmana and Rama, back to back, swung their swords with such might and precision that they lopped off the fearsome heads of their attackers. From the severed necks of the demons there came a spout of green slime that splattered into the air and rained down upon the princely brothers.

In the midst of this hard-won victory of the monkeys, there came a disaster. The battle suddenly turned against them. Sampathi, swooping down upon the demons who guarded Sita in her garden prison, was struck by three arrows. He desperately flapped his wide wings, trying to stay aloft, but his life gushed from him like blood. He came crashing down on the ramparts of the palace, and his glorious plumes burst into flames.

When the warriors saw Sampathi wounded, Jambavan and his army of bears rushed toward the garden to rescue Sita, only to be met by a deluge of arrows so mutilating that it forced them to take cover behind the black rocks that formed the walls of Sita's prison.

At the same moment, a demon, mad with rage, screamed and turned his chariot at full speed into Hanuman, tearing open the ape's powerful chest. For an instant, Hanuman fell back in shock and pain. But then he grasped his gaping wound and pulled it closed with his bare hands as he sprang at the hurtling chariot that had mutilated him. With a wild shout Hanuman raised his fist and brought it down upon the chariot with such force that the charioteer dissolved into vile slime and the war wagon burst into splinters.

At the sight of Hanuman's reprisal, triumphant shouts arose from the monkeys and bears. And, encouraged by Hanuman's bravery, the creatures of the forest renewed their deadly battle against the demons.

Then something happened. There came a sudden hush as the two lethal enemies fell silent and slowly backed away from each other. The demons and the monkeys peered up into the air in awe and dread. For into the melee came a towering shadow, striding menacingly forward and surrounded by ten thousand flitting bats and twenty thousand growling fiends armed with darts that writhed like snakes and lances that tore at the flesh like vicious teeth.

In the flickering light of the smoldering fires Rama could see that the enormous and looming figure was the demon king himself. *Ravana.*

In the harrowing silence, Laksmana quickly drew his sword.

"No!" cried Rama.

But it was too late. His valiant young brother had already rushed toward the monumental demon king, swinging his weapon with all his might.

"Stand clear of him!" shouted Rama, drawing an arrow against the string of his magic bow and aiming it at Ravana's claws, which held a wriggling serpent anxious to feed on Laksmana's spirit.

But Laksmana would not stop. He was so filled with the aspiration of achieving a victory that would be a credit to his father and his older brother that he did not hear Rama's warnings.

"Ravana is mine!" Laksmana bellowed, leaping high into the air and plunging his sword into Ravana's breast.

Rama anxiously aimed his arrow, but he could not let it fly while Laksmana still hung in midair, clutching the handle of his sword.

"Jump!" shouted Hanuman.

"Leave your sword and jump!" cried Rama.

But Laksmana would not let go of his sword that was so deeply lodged in the demon's chest that it could not be tugged loose.

Laksmana's legs dangled in the air as Ravana tossed back and forth, trying to shake off his attacker.

Then, with a piercing wail, Laksmana began to fall, plummeting to the ground with such force that his strong legs collapsed under him and the bones shattered.

Desperate to save his brother, Rama dropped his bow and raced toward Laksmana.

The demon king laughed mockingly.

"What a pity," came the hoarse growl of Ravana as he leered down at Laksmana, "that such a courageous effort is wasted! But as you see, young warrior, I am unharmed and your miserable little life has been squandered on conceit, because Ravana does not have a heart!"

With those words, the demon king plucked the sword from his chest and began to laugh his horrible laughter, tilting back his head in perverse delight as sparks and smoke poured from his twisted and crimson mouth.

In that moment Rama lunged for his brother in the hope of pulling him to safety while the demon was distracted. But seeing Rama's desperate effort to save his brother, Ravana fell deathly silent. Then, just as Rama came within arm's reach of his defenseless brother, Ravana slowly lifted his ponderous foot and brought it down with a thunderous roar upon Laksmana.

For a moment the young man's body squirmed in agony. His head fell back, a look of astonishment filling his handsome face. Blood trickled from his nostrils as he fought to stay whole, but his insides began to seep from the terrible wound in his belly. He groaned and clutched at his innards as he rolled upon the ground. Then the bright light in his eyes suddenly went out. And he died.

Rama's spirit was utterly crushed by the sight of his brother's maimed body. He fell back in grief and remorse, drained of courage as tears streamed down his face. He opened his mouth to call his brother's name, but no sound came from his throat.

Now there was only silence.

The monkey army recoiled in dismay and sorrow at the sight of the dead Laksmana and the grief-stricken Rama.

While Ravana gloated and chuckled, his army of demons slid like snails into the shadows of the interior of the palace.

On a signal from the demon king, his army completely vanished.

Silence now, except for the sobs of Lord Rama and the soft, voluptuous laughter of the demon king as he slowly faded from sight.

For a moment, the monkeys remained absolutely motionless, alert lest the demons suddenly renewed their attack. But when it became clear that the monsters had retreated into the safety of their fortress, the animals slowly crept toward Rama, murmuring in distress and confusion.

King Sugriva knelt beside Rama, nodding in profound sorrow.

Hanuman and Angada slowly approached Laksmana's broken body, and then they fell to their knees and wept.

There was a deathly silence in the littered battlefield. Nothing stirred.

No one spoke.

Only the lonely sigh of the hot wind and the growling of the angry clouds. The continual pelting of the bloody rain.

Then Rama peered angrily into the black mist that Ravana had left behind him, a trail of blood and ashes like a blotch on the earth. Through the broken gates and crumbled walls Rama could see nothing. Not a trace of the enemy. Ravana and his horde had vanished into a mist.

Nothing moved in the smoldering ruins.

Only whistling wind and the faint cry of dying creatures somewhere in the distance.

Rama embraced his brother's body with great tenderness, cradling it in his arms. Then the look of grief in the prince's eyes slowly changed, and a terrible wrath flooded his face. He arose wearily and gazed in anguish at Laksmana's twisted corpse as the monkeys gently bore the body to the water's edge.

As his brother was carried away, Rama mournfully stared across the deathly landscape that stretched endlessly into the gloom. The carnage was numbing. Everywhere were the headless corpses of monkeys. The

shattered carcasses of bears. The broken bodies of birds.
Smashed chariots littered the battlefield. Ruined walls.
Seething fires. Bloody lances and demolished swords.
Weapons piled everywhere. Blood flowing everywhere.
Countless demons lay rotting and seething in heaps,
dissolving into thick sludge that oozed over the forsaken
land. Even great Sampathi lay dead upon the high ram-
parts of the palace where he had collapsed.

"Now . . ." muttered Rama in a voice full of frustration
and rage, "I myself go to confront Ravana!"

Alone and without an ally, Rama strode fearlessly into
the dank interior of Ravana's palace.

The animals crept cautiously behind him, while
Hanuman and Angada lumbered bravely at Rama's side,
carrying his arrows and his magic bow.

What the warriors found in the court of Ravana was so
ghastly that the entire assembly was struck dumb.

Within the sunless courtyard were lines of starving
farmers and their children. Swaying listlessly back and
forth, trying to stay on their feet lest they be whipped
and beaten by their captors. Their faces were blank and
their hollow eyes were fixed in an expression of horror
and pain.

Rama made his way forlornly between the prisoners,
gazing in shock and misery at the horrifying interior of
the fortress.

Amidst the cobwebs and mud and slime, masses of
gems and gold were carelessly piled. Everywhere were

baskets brimming with bloody feathers and once-elegant plumes. Heaps of rotting fruits and vegetables were dumped in the gutters of the courtyard. Everything the good earth had once produced in abundance had been confiscated by the demons and left to rot.

In the dark corners were clusters of naked peasant women, sprawled in misery on the filthy floor, their backs and legs raw from the beatings they had long endured. High above, on the ramparts and stone stairways of the fortress, long lines of wrecked men and beasts staggered through the dimness, bent under the burden of large stones they carried on their backs.

Thrown and piled everywhere were the heads of creatures: tigers and bears, elephants and monkeys. And on every wall were countless cages filled with birds that beat their wings frantically against the bars.

Clogging the foul cistern of the courtyard, where fresh water had once flowed, there were now the half-devoured bodies of every animal that had ever lived in the peace and greenery of beautiful Lanka's springtimes, before the land had been murdered by the invading demons.

The mighty armies of King Sugriva were so stunned and horrified by what they found within the vile court of Ravana that their weary and blood-smeared faces streamed with a million bitter tears.

With wretched cries of alarm, the heroic troops of birds that had fought the demons with beaks and claws fluttered anxiously into the gloom, darting from one wall to the next as they lovingly released their kinfolk from their miserable cages.

The grieved commander Jambavan and his loyal troops of bears sprawled hopelessly upon the ground and searched into the dead eyes of the piles of severed heads, sighing and weeping as they recognized friends and loved ones who had been seized and stolen from the forest by the demons of Lanka.

Everywhere was the sound of sighs and weeping among the staunchest of warriors.

But Hanuman, blood still gushing from his wound, refused to be defeated by grief. With the pounding of his feet he bellowed in outrage. Then Angada joined Hanuman in a thunderous battle cry. The whimpering and moaning ceased. And the mournful warriors raised themselves from their misery and wildly pursued the demons with many shouts and curses.

When they finally came upon their sequestered enemies, who had fled into Ravana's innermost court, the monkeys and bears were so driven by outrage for the murder of their kinsmen that they threw themselves upon the demons, without concern for whether they themselves lived or died, biting and clawing their way through the gruesome ranks of demons as they gradually fought closer and closer to King Ravana.

Blood gushed into the air and flesh spattered in every direction. Dying animals and dying demons screamed and writhed upon the courtyard floor. But still the battle did not end, so mad with grief were the creatures of the forest that they would make any sacrifice in order to lay their claws upon the demon king who towered over them, shaking with wicked laughter and delighted by the bloodbath raging all around him.

Ravana's laughter echoed through the fetid halls of his fortress until, suddenly, Rama fearlessly strode through the doorway of the inner court. Then the demon's laughter vanished, and he nervously summoned his sentinels to defend him. But the battle had grown so fierce that Ravana's guardians did not hear his command.

Rama's face was set in an expression of such fury that even King Ravana, the most evil of all things evil, could not look into his eyes. And when Rama deliberately raised his bow and aimed an arrow at the wicked king, Ravana turned in fear and made his escape up the long stairway leading to the wide ramparts at the summit of the fortress.

Rama rushed after the fleeing demon, oblivious to everything but the immense pain of his brother's death.

Leaping the long rows of steps that led to the uppermost levels of the fortress, Rama was driven by a burning energy so great that he seemed to fly in the air above the endless stairways that jutted out from the steep walls of the courtyard.

Finally Rama burst into the open air, where he dashed headlong over the wide ramparts that towered so high above the earth that the ground below was shrouded in darkness.

Rama ran first in one direction and then another in search of his enemy. But Ravana was nowhere to be found.

Just as Rama was about to abandon his quest and rejoin his warriors in the courtyard below, he heard a pebble fall from the ruined tower of the fortress. Then a stone slipped from the crumbling walls and plunged downward to the ground far below.

Rama cautiously drew his bow and peered into the bloody rain and the dimness that lay along the summit of the fortress. For a moment he did not move, but then he carefully crept toward a narrow ledge circling precariously the base of the collapsed tower. When another stone slipped into space, Rama became certain that the demon king was hiding on the far side of the fallen turret.

Rama silently drew from his quiver a fiery arrow, which hissed in anticipation of its flight like a serpent coiling in preparation to spring upon a victim. Then he carefully placed the arrow against the string of his powerful bow. It was an arrow of terrifying magic. In its wings was the wild wind and in its point glowed the furnace of the sun.

With his weapon in hand, Rama edged his way onto the narrow ledge jutting out from the crumbled tower, pressing his back against the wall lest he plunge into the awful abyss that loomed beneath him.

Moving one foot at a time, Rama shuffled cautiously around the tower as its stones became dislodged by his weight and bits of the ledge snapped and fell into a resounding emptiness.

Then in the gloom Rama saw the glowing crimson of the demon's eyes.

"Stay away! I am defenseless," whimpered Ravana.

"There is no pity in the world for one as wicked as you!" cried Rama as he stretched his bow with full force, ready to send the arrow into the monster's head.

"How can you slay a warrior without weapons?" Ravana whined as his shifty eyes sought some object or weapon with which he could destroy Rama.

"Whether you have a weapon or not, it matters little to me. Laksmana is dead. And now, Lord Ravana, you too are dead."

Enraged by the thought of his brother's death, Rama pulled harder on the string of his bow, but just as he was about to let his magic arrow fly, Ravana lunged at him, toppling Rama from the lofty ledge upon which he was balanced.

Rama cried out as he lost his footing. He began to plummet into space. But as he slid to his knees and began to tumble into the empty darkness, he frantically twisted his body toward Ravana, and with a final shout of defiance, he let his deadly arrow fly. No sooner had the arrow burst into the air than Rama desperately grabbed for the crumbling ledge as he plunged past it, barely catching hold of a sturdy stone truss that broke his fall.

As Rama hung helplessly in the air, the long screech of the mortally wounded Ravana resounded through the heavens. For a moment the terrible demon tottered upon the ledge above Rama, clutching the bloody gash where the magic arrow had pierced his skull.

"What a world! What a world!" Ravana groaned in astonishment and pain. "Who would have thought that a mere mortal could destroy my beautiful wickedness!"

Ravana stumbled to one side and blindly grappled for a handhold. Then his gaping wound began to sputter and fume, sending out a gush of putrid slime and clusters of black spiders and writhing worms.

For a moment he seemed to be frozen in the darkness of the sky. Then he teetered forward and slowly plummeted into empty space.

"Look out! Look out!" he screamed to the jagged rocks of the decimated earth that hungered for him. "I am dying!"

When Ravana struck the ground, Rama heard a piercing scream that seemed to come from a very great distance. It was the outcry of someone he vaguely recalled from his last sad days under the roof of his father, but he did not realize that it was the scream of the evil young queen Kekay-yee.

From the seething blood and gore of Ravana's crushed body flowed a river of tears. And as that river flowed over the wasteland that had once been beautiful Lanka, tender seedlings began to break through the sterile soil. Leaves burst from the barren bark of the lifeless trees. And from everywhere came a mysterious sound.

Prince Rama dragged himself to the safety of the fortress ledge and breathlessly peered down at the colossal hulk of Ravana's disintegrating corpse.

Now he stood in silence as, far below, the monkeys and bears and birds wildly performed a dance of victory around the body of the slain demon.

But Rama could not join in the celebration. He sighed as he thought of the death of Laksmana and Sampathi. The battle had crushed his spirit. But he became heartened when he realized that Sita was awaiting him in her prison garden.

"Sita," he murmured.

With the sound of Sita's name, the moonless sky once again filled with moonlight. From everywhere came a mysterious sound. It arose from the sorrowful earth where the demon's flesh dissolved and trickled among the rocks, forming streams that ran into a vast river filled to its depths with long-forgotten animal dreams and mortal memories.

The sound from the earth was a strange and muffled song, drifting upward . . . rising like a distant echo from the naked, steaming soil. The song lingered in the night's moonlit breeze, carrying aloft the everlasting fragrance of birth and death and eternal renewal.

The Throne

Here now in his triumph where all things falter,
Stretched out on the spoils that his own hand spread,
As a god self-slain on his own strange altar,
Death lies dead.

—Algernon Charles Swinburne

Twenty

A FRESH, STRONG GUST of wind whirled through the coronation chamber, bringing with it, like leaves in a storm, countless sentries and nobles, priests and curious creatures that were neither mortals nor animals. A bright, crystalline music resounded. Cloud bells and lightning cymbals crackled and clattered, filling the air with their clamor. The massive walls of the palace of Dasaratha slowly glistened, becoming as translucent as glass and allowing a torrent of dazzling sunlight to flood the throne room.

Everywhere there were the excited voices of the countless beings who had mysteriously appeared. But when Rama raised his arms, they respectfully lowered to their knees and fell silent.

"I bid you to sound the drums and to inform the priests to bring forth the most sacred of things in our kingdom!" Rama exclaimed. "Bring me the container of the Tiger Bow, that it may go back to rest in its bed and so peace

209

may once again come to the world! For now it is time for me to bid farewell to my weapon and my friend in battle. For it was this weapon that saved my life and slayed Lord Ravana. And it was this weapon whose unyielding strength yielded to me when I won the gift of Sita!"

An exuberant shout rang out from the crowd. People threw brightly colored blossoms and fragrant rice into the air. The drums roared as the priests spilled precious wine upon the stone floor, marking the path of a procession of petite temple dancers, wrapped in rich gold brocades and adorned with flowers and jewels. Their long slender fingers undulated as they floated forward and their eyes were glazed and spellbound. Their gorgeous headdresses were fashioned from wreaths of silver, festooned with frangipani blooms and dangling with tinkling bells.

Then the trance dancers careened through the crowd, snarling and wheeling hypnotically as they thrust their ivory-crowned daggers into their breasts, opening wide but bloodless wounds.

Everywhere there was shimmering music and the ceaseless chanting of men: "*Ait! Aes, aes, byok, sirrr! Cak . . . cak . . . cuk!*"

Then came long processions of women carrying tall, swaying pennants made of palm leaves and orchid garlands, followed by the honored elders holding lofty silken umbrellas wrapped in saffron cloth and colored raffia.

At the end of the long procession were five hundred burly men who staggered forward, barely able to draw the eight-wheeled cart on which was carried the iron box that was the resting place of the Tiger Bow. The crowd coaxed the men onward. And in response to the urging of the honored assembly they brayed and groaned as they made renewed efforts to wheel the cart into the presence of Prince Rama.

At last it was achieved. A priest stepped solemnly forward and opened the large iron box, stepping aside so Rama could gently set the marvelous weapon back in its resting place.

But before Rama would release the magic bow from his grasp, he turned solemnly to the vast gathering of richly costumed celebrants and well-wishers. And then, in a dark voice, he said, "Before there can be peace, however, I must first see the woman who conspired to send me into exile and who connived to steal my throne."

Nervous whispers fluttered among the guests.

"Before I lay down my weapon," Rama continued in a wrathful voice, "I must come face to face with that young wife of my dear father. And I must see her son for whom she claimed my place at my father's side!"

A fearful hush fell upon the assembly.

"Where is Kekay-yee?" Rama thundered. "Where is she now that I have returned? What has become of her deceitful smiles? Where are her cunning laughter and girlish sighs?"

The crowd stirred with anxiety and apprehension, fearing that even the coronation of their new king would bring bloodshed.

"Tell me now!" shouted Rama. "Where is that deceitful woman who broke my father's heart? And where is the son for whom she claimed my throne?"

Now the dancers ceased to dance. Now the music ended.

So great was the anger in Rama's voice that no one spoke or moved.

"*Bring me Kekay-yee!*" bellowed Rama. "How dare she miss this coronation she so wickedly sought for her own son! Bring her to me if she lacks the courage to face me without being dragged to my feet!"

The guests recoiled from Rama's wrath, stepping aside as a terrible old hag stumbled between them and hobbled toward the prince.

"Your warriors need not drag me to your throne," the hag muttered in a failing voice full of spite and malice. "I have lost. Look at me! I grow older by the moment and have no will to fight for my miserable life."

Rama gazed at the battered old woman with suspicion and surprise.

"Kekay-yee?" he murmured in disbelief. "Is it truly you? Could my father's youthful bride be this ancient hag?"

Kekay-yee teetered back and forth, barely able to stand. Even as Rama stared at her, her skin wrinkled and crumpled and she continued to shrink into the ground.

Her royal robe slipped from her haggard shoulders. Her once-glistening eyes had become gray and lightless. And her once-delicate hands had become gnarled and bony. Kekay-yee was wasting away.

"What has happened to you?" Rama muttered as an expression of pity filled his face.

"You destroyed Ravana," Kekay-yee moaned. "And when you killed the demon king you also killed me, for he was the keeper of my spirit."

"And your son? Where is the son you promised my father?"

"There is no son," Kekay-yee hissed as she wheezed and coughed and a malicious glint came into her pitiless eyes. "I lied. Anything to keep you from your father's throne! I lied! There never was a son!"

"No son?" Rama muttered in pained astonishment. "You had no son and yet you sent Laksmana into exile to die! You had no child and yet you sent Sita into the clutches of a demon! Could it be true? Did you do such wicked things just for the power of my father's throne?"

Kekay-yee smiled wickedly. "To take what is not mine," she muttered darkly, her vacant eyes filling with a savage satisfaction. "To turn good into evil. To bring down a hero. And to deliver Ravana from his eternal darkness into the failing light of Dasaratha!"

Rama recoiled from her terrible words.

But Kekay-yee laughed in his face with a terrible madness. "You would like to know why pain and evil exists in your perfect world," she gloated as a fierce fire came into her pitiless eyes. "You would like to know why you sicken and die!" she howled with a vicious delight. "But for little people like you, who dream of happiness, there can never be a lesson in a story that ends happily!"

With these words Kekay-yee scoffed at Rama and opened her mouth in a ghastly, toothless smile.

"Then it is your turn for banishment!" exclaimed Rama, gesturing to the guards to seize Kekay-yee.

"It is too late for banishment," the hag wheezed with a sinister laugh. "It is far too late for heroic gestures! I am dead already. When you killed Ravana, you killed my husband! For I was the bride of the demon king long before I came to your miserable father's bed. And when you killed my husband, you also killed my fondest dream of putting evil upon your father's throne, where Ravana and I could have ruled together over a world of beautiful wickedness! But now all is lost for me. I am melting even as you watch me speak. A creature without a spirit cannot survive for long . . . not even a demon."

With these words, Kekay-yee's shrinking body began to glisten and glow. From her wrinkled mouth sprang the terrible fangs of a demon. From her eyes flashed the fearsome crimson leer of a fiend. Her flesh began to dissolve, revealing the ghastly scales of a monster. And as she slowly shriveled and sank into the floor, she gasped.

"Ravana! Ravana! Where is my spirit? What have you done with it?"

Then she was gone.

In the astonished silence of the assembly, Prince Rama lovingly placed the mysterious bow into its resting place.

"Now let there be springtime in our kingdom!" he declared. "Let us greet the return of life to the living!"

An exuberant shout rang out from the crowd. Once again the happy people of Dasaratha and Janaka threw brightly colored blossoms and fragrant rice into the air. The drums roared and the temple dancers resumed their delicate dances. Their long slender fingers flickered in the sunlight as they floated forward amidst the sound of a thousand tinkling bells.

Rama's mother, Kowsalya, who had been a captive in her chamber during her son's long exile, rushed to him, and with tearful joy she kissed and embraced him. A jubilant cheer went up when the elderly queen took her place beside her princely son. Then the drums thundered and the trumpets blared as the throng at the coronation saluted their new young king.

With a grave gesture of honor and abdication, old king Janaka embraced Rama. Then, bowing to the young prince, he removed the crown from his head and placed it in Rama's hands.

The holiest priests of both Dasaratha and Janaka stepped slowly forward to the beat of the ritual music. And when Rama solemnly took his place upon the throne of both Dasaratha and Janaka, the high priest ceremonially placed a bejeweled crown of both kingdoms upon

Rama's head. With a whimsical smile King Janaka placed his delicate evergreen scepter upon Rama's lap.

Then as the music resounded throughout the kingdoms of Dasaratha and Janaka the people began to sing and dance. They threw clouds of blossoms and rice into the candlelit air, rejoicing that the winter had ended and springtime had come once again.

Long processions of loyal subjects paraded before King Rama, bringing many precious gifts. And everywhere was the sound of laughter and music and revelry.

As Rama sat upon his throne, greeting his subjects, there came a sudden breeze. It swept over the courtyard with a marvelous fragrance. Then there came a cascade of warmth, and all at once Lord Rama could hear the sound of grass singing its long green song. He could hear the rustle of blossoms bursting into bloom. The ancient sigh of lands and rivers.

"Silence," King Rama commanded as he stood and intently peered around him, listening to the sounds of the earth singing to him.

It was a strange, muffled song: drifting upward, rising like a distant echo from the naked stones of the palace.

In the song-filled air, the vibrant sun veiled itself with silvery clouds. Then, in the dimness, a warm shadow drifted into the chamber . . . a slender figure slowly emerging from the soft green mist that hovered in the air.

Rama gasped with delight and wonder.

"Sita!"

Standing before him was his wife.

Rama gazed at her with great longing. She glistened like a lotus just opening in the evening; rising above the calm water upon the pedestal of one perfectly oval leaf; her white flesh, her flawless body, and her enchanting face crowned by long tresses of emerald hair.

Sita smiled at her husband as she hovered in the green mist that surrounded her, swaying gently as crystal chimes resounded in cascades of shimmering music. She was close but far, her eyes glazed and her glance remote, looking out at the world as if she were not quite a part of it.

"My husband . . ." Sita murmured, with a loving smile for Rama. "My beloved father," she whispered as she kissed the old king on his brow. "My dearest mother," she sighed as she came forward and bowed to the dowager queen Kowsalya.

The great assembly glanced adoringly at their young queen as she took her place at her husband's side.

Then in the stillness she whispered, "Look, dear Rama. See the coronation gift I have brought for you! It is not grand or costly. And it is neither gold nor silver. And yet it is the only gift I have for you. It is as fragile as snow. As tender as a blade of grass. And yet it is as powerful as the wind. Come, Rama, come see what I have here in my hand for you."

Sita slowly opened her hand, and in her narrow palm Rama was surprised to see a tiny seed.

"Ah," murmured Rama in wonderment. "Tell me, dear Sita, what is this curious gift that you have brought to me?"

Sita smiled radiantly as clouds rolled across her brow and a silver rain fell upon her head. She laughed ever so gently as the darkness of the twilight began to fill her glimmering eyes with moonlight, and sprouts and blossoms sprang slowly from her flawless flesh.

"My husband," she whispered as the wind carried the cosmic seed into the everlasting sky, "this thing I give you . . . it is called life."

And then, as suddenly as night had fallen, a bright new dawn made its way into the springtime sky. A bright yellow bird darted into the air. Flitting in the mist. Beaming. Brightly gleaming. While from the distance came the ever-trilling song of life.

Singing.

The Storyteller's Farewell

How the Story Was Born

WHEN THE STORY IS FINISHED, there is usually very little more to tell. But for me there were so many adventures that led to the writing of this book that I have felt compelled to write an epilogue so I can tell the additional story of how this novel came to be written.

The inspiration for the book came from a long literary work called *Ramayana,* one of the central epics of India and Southeast Asia. The original story consists of 24,000 verses that date back to the first century B.C. It is a series of tales about the many adventures of Prince Rama. Those tales have been told and retold for over two thousand years. They have been used as the basis of many dramas, films, dances, and operas. And for me the *Ramayana* is also a saga that begs to be retold in a modern novel because it is so ideally suited to my love of fantastic literature and because of my interests in the way people understand themselves and their world through the marvelous stories and beliefs they call their mythology.

In writing this book, however, I did not wish simply to retell an ancient legend. I wanted to use that legend as the springboard for my own imagination and for my own songs of destiny. In this way, this novel has become a part of my own mythology.

The story is ancient, but the words are new. The characters are known to every man, woman, and child in India and Indonesia, but I have reimagined the extraordinary adventures of these famous heroes in terms of my own visions and my own fancies.

Though I have long known and admired the *Ramayana*, the experience that finally prompted me to write this novel was my several visits to India and Southeast Asia. Of all the exotic lands I have visited in my continual travels around the world, none compares to what I discovered among those beautiful Hindu people who live on the enchanted little island called Bali.

It was on that marvelous island that I witnessed trance dances and fantastic dramatic rituals. In Bali, I heard the voices of the singers and the stories of chanters and the music of gamelan orchestras composed of drums and gongs and every other imaginable metallic instrument. I heard the marvelous tales of Lord Rama told and reenacted by the dancers and actors who sustain Bali's living traditions. I watched the endless exercises and difficult training of fabulous performers, some no older than eight or nine years. And when I finally left Bali, I was so deeply touched by its living legends and its sense of reverence for all things of the earth that I wanted to find a way of giving tribute to the remarkable people and culture I had encountered during my time on Bali.

So this novel is my homage to the exceptional experiences I was given during my ventures into the world and into the lives of the Balinese people.

I am by no means the first person in the arts to be fascinated by Bali. In the 1920s and 1930s, many writers and artists visited the island. One of them was a Russian-born artist of German heritage by the name of Walter Spies, who came to live in Bali in the 1930s because, I suspect, he was attracted by the same indefinable allure that brought me there.

Walter Spies loved the Balinese people and they loved him. And by the time he was forced to flee from Bali because of the invasion by the Imperial Japanese Army at the onset of World War II, he had made a profound and lasting impact on the arts of Bali, and the Balinese people had made an equally strong impact on his life and art.

What Spies discovered in Bali is what I also discovered. Everywhere I traveled, I encountered an expression of the sacredness of nature that is such a fundamental aspect of Balinese life it has become an inseparable part of the daily life of the people.

In the unique paintings, sculptures, rituals, and

dramatic dances that are a constant and central part of the lives of the people of every village, I witnessed a reverence for both the ferocity and gentleness of the universe. I also witnessed a love of the arts that makes an impact on every moment of the lives of the towns and villages.

As I trekked among the rice terraces and into the mountains and along the wide and wonderful coastlines, I found a world of abundant wildlife, fantastic plants, and angry volcanoes. But most important for me, I also encountered a remarkable and gentle people unlike any I have found anywhere else on earth, so secure in the reality of themselves that they were unafraid of outsiders.

Miraculously I found all of these adventures and experiences on a tiny island tossed in the turbulent currents of the South China Sea that flow endlessly into the Sea of Java. I found a fragile speck of land called Bali that rises above the tempestuous waves. And what I discovered astonished me with its bewitching and vivid culture . . . a culture born in the deeply rooted myths and ceremonies of a religious idealism that flourishes in every thought and every activity of the lives of the extraordinary and ordinary people of the island.

Bali is alive, and yet it has become a haven for something that has vanished from the rest of the world. And when I encountered that rare and vivid preserve of mystery and enchantment, I knew that I had to find some way of using my skills as a writer to share my experience with others.

Like Walter Spies, I have come away from Bali forever changed. That personal transformation is mirrored in this book. I wanted to re-create my experience of Bali by creating my own response to what I found in the lives and myths of the people of that tiny Southeast Asian island of magic. I wanted to memorialize the adoration of the creative and destructive forces of nature that I found there.

The result of my efforts is a curious blend of many of my experiences of Balinese culture as well as my experiences of my own life in America. And so this novel is filled with images of jungles, temples, demons, heroes, talking animals, and dancing gods. And it is also filled with the echoes of magic from my own childhood: including European fairy tales, stories of American Indians, and even the marvelous tale of *The Wizard of Oz*, from which I borrowed those famous last words of the Wicked Witch and put them into the mouth of Ravana, the terrible demon king of Lanka.

I have said it before but I must say it again. Not many of us are willing to sail away to strange worlds that challenge the truths and beliefs of our own familiar world. But for those who are willing to step beyond the gates of their walled cities, a great adventure can be found.

A French poet once said: For those who are walled up, everything is a wall . . . even an open door.

I always try to see the open door, for there are worlds out there that ever beckon to us with the promise of exceptional discoveries.

Open the gates! Do not be afraid of what you are becoming. Dare yourself to answer the call! For in discovering the unexpected, you are bound to discover yourself!

Jamake Highwater
Los Angeles, California, 1994